"Your last name is Clark?"

Katie's attention shifted back to the man. Why was he so focused on her last name? She nodded. "Yes, Katie Clark."

"Short for Kathleen."

A sense of foreboding slid through her, as if caring for the train-wreck victims wouldn't be her greatest challenge in the coming days. However did this man know her Christian name, and more important, why?

"You don't remember me, do you, Katie Bug?"

Katie gasped. There was only one person who'd ever used that silly name for her, a boy, no more than eighteen the last time she'd seen him. That had been seven years ago, right after her mother had died. What was he doing here now, when she had finally forged a life for herself?

"Katie, are you okay? Who is this man?" Woody asked from his place beside her, concern lacing his voice.

"Let me introduce myself." The gentleness in his expression had taken on a hard edge as he glared at Katie before turning his attention back to Woody. "I'm Dr. Joshua McClain, Katie's fiancé."

Books by Patty Smith Hall

Love Inspired Heartsong Presents

The Doctor's Bride

Love Inspired Historical

Hearts in Flight
Hearts in Hiding

PATTY SMITH HALL

A Georgia girl born and bred, Patty Smith Hall loves to incorporate little-known historical facts into her stories. Her writing goal is to create characters who walk the Christian walk despite their human flaws. When she's not writing, Patty enjoys spending time with her husband of twenty-eight years, their two daughters and a vast extended family.

Patty loves hearing from her readers! Please contact her through her website, www.pattysmithhall.com.

PATTY SMITH HALL

The Doctor's Bride

Recycling programs for this product may not exist in your area.

ISBN-13: 978-0-373-48681-6

THE DOCTOR'S BRIDE

This edition published by arrangement with Love Inspired Books.

www.Harlequin.com

Printed in U.S.A.

To every thing there is a season,
and a time to every purpose under the heaven.
—*Ecclesiastes* 3:1

To my grandma, Ruth Rogers Clark. I love you.

To Laurie Alice, Gina and Pamela—thank you
for allowing me this opportunity to work with
such a talented and wonderful group! I am humbled.

Chapter 1

Near Hillsdale, Michigan
1856

Dr. Joshua McClain stared out the glass window at the blur of endless white, his exhalation frosting over the clear pane into a swirling icy cloud. The gentle rocking of the train might have coaxed him into sleep, but he'd never seen snow like this in his home state of South Carolina, turning the night into an eerie shade of gray. An ethereal mist held the passenger car in a tight cocoon, leaving him with an unsettling feeling of loneliness.

Angling his black felt hat over his eyes, Josh nestled deeper into his new wool coat, shrugging off the feeling. Wasn't that what he wanted, to be as far away from the hustle and bustle of Charleston, from debutantes and their marriage-minded mamas who only saw him as a means to his father's supposed vast fortune? From Samuel McClain himself and his misguided ideas about Josh's chosen profession? No, the uncharted Kansas Territory now held his destiny, while the only tie binding him to the past was in some forsaken place called Hillsdale, Michigan.

Katie Clark. His childhood friend had invaded his thoughts often over the past seven years—the way her eyes sparkled in delight at the simplest pleasure, her determination to care for the sick and mistreated animals they'd come across in their youthful adventures. Good memories. Wonderful memories.

But nothing to base a marriage on.

Why on earth had his father sold him off to the highest bidder, agreeing to a marriage contract with the last person he expected?

Josh shivered and stuffed his frozen hands into his coat pockets, the rabbit-fur lining offering little relief from the cold. Had the temperature dropped another degree, or was it the chill he always felt whenever his thoughts strayed to Katie ever since his father had showed him the contract? It didn't matter. The situation would soon be settled when he got to Hillsdale. All he wanted now was a warm bed and a hot meal.

"Dr. McClain?"

Josh turned, squinting into the near black, barely making out the shadowy silhouette of the conductor. "Yes?"

"The porter wanted me to inform you he has secured the new equipment in the trunks you provided."

"Good." The new microscope and surgical instruments Josh had acquired in Chicago would come in handy once his office, along with a living space out back, was completed. Excitement at the prospect of being his own boss rose up inside him, then tapered. He'd feel better once this unfinished business with Katie and her father was settled. "How long until we reach Hillsdale?"

The man sighed, as if the question had been one he'd heard repeated often during the course of the evening. "We're just a mile or two outside of town, sir. You should be able to see the lights of the station coming up in a few moments."

The conductor had moved past Josh, but the manners ingrained in him by his mother prevailed. "Thank…"

The sharp vibrato of the train whistle split the night air. Before Josh could form the question in his mind, his world shifted off center, the passenger car skating along the top of the rails like the children he'd watched earlier today, sliding over the thick lake ice on sharpened blades of steel. The high-pitched scream of metal against metal pierced the dark, sending sparks of unidentifiable sound rippling against the walls.

The train car tilted hard to the left, slamming it on its side, throwing Josh against the window. Tiny droplets—fire? ice?—rained down on him, stinging his face and the exposed skin of his neck. Instinctively, he folded his arms over his head, his eyes squeezed painfully shut as his mother's gentle instruction to pray took hold.

Lord, have I come all this way to begin my life, only to lose it?

The unearthly grinding stopped, holding Josh suspended for just a moment before the sound of shattering glass rang in his ears. He grasped the bench in front of him, digging his fingers into the broken wood, trying to focus his scattered thoughts. How many people had been in the passenger car with him? Most of the passengers had disembarked in Adrian, choosing to ride out the storm in the comfort of a warm bed rather than pressing on. But the few left would need immediate attention. *Father God, please let me live long enough to help those around me.*

A low-pitched moan from just in front of him jerked him out of his prayer, the metallic smell of cooling metal filling the car. Josh ran his tongue over his lips, tasting blood.

He had to get out of there—that was, if he could move. Stretching his legs out, Josh held his breath, waiting for the first twinge of pain that would signal a broken bone, then he tested his arms. Maybe a few cuts and scrapes, but nothing major. Slowly, he sat up. With barely any light, he couldn't see his hand in front of his face, much less the injured or dying.

But he could offer comfort. "Hello?"

A slight whimper came from the front of the railcar. A child maybe? Or a young girl? "Hello?"

Several moments ticked by before a childish voice wobbled out a reply. "Yes?"

Josh frowned. A girl, probably no more than seven or eight years old from the sound of her. Just about the age Katie Clark had been the first time he'd met her, on the front porch of his father's Abbeville plantation. He squashed the memory. "Are you hurt?"

"My arm hurts, but I can move it." She hesitated for a moment. "Are you G-G-G-God?"

The question caught him off guard. Poor kid must have been scared to death. "I'm Dr. McClain. And who might you be?"

"My name is Ginger, like the spice."

In spite of their predicament, Josh's lips twitched upward into a slight smile. Maybe if he could keep her talking, he could track her whereabouts and at least sit with her until help came. "How old are you, Ginger?"

"Nine, on my next birthday."

"Nine, huh?" Easing himself onto his knees, Josh stretched his hands along the wall, vaguely surprised that the varnished siding hadn't splintered in the roll. His fingers met resistance in his next movement forward, a rise of an inch or so. The window, he reasoned, sliding to the left until his shoulder brushed against what once was the roof. "Why, you'd almost be considered a lady back where I come from!"

He breathed a bit easier when she replied with a hint of laughter in her voice. "Dr. Clark told me the last time I came to visit that I'll be taller than my aunt before you know it."

Josh froze. "You know the doctor?"

"Everyone in Hillsdale knows Dr. Clark. Aunt Elizabeth—she's the principal over the lady students at the college—is always saying there's no finer person in all the world than Dr. Clark."

Josh grimaced as he slid forward. Dr. Clark's actions didn't impress him as those of an honorable man. After all, what kind of man purchased a husband for his daughter, offering his desperate father silver in exchange for Josh's future? Their fathers should have been more practical, not that either man had ever been particularly prudent when it came to their wives or their pocketbooks. A dull ache settled in Josh's chest. Maybe if his father had been more sensible, Mother wouldn't have been at the reins when her buggy flipped, taking her and Millicent Clark to an early grave.

Josh sighed. What was done was done. He finally had his medical degree and a little money to set up his practice out West. A marriage contract wasn't going to stop Josh from taking control of his own life.

"Are you still there, Dr. McClain?"

Josh pushed his thoughts aside and moved forward. "I'm here, sweetheart."

She released a relieved breath. "Good. I thought something had happened to you."

He cringed at the thought of distressing this child even more than she already was. "So, tell me, why did you ask if I were God?"

"Aunt Elizabeth says the Lord speaks in a still small voice." The child hesitated for a moment. "I haven't ever heard Him, so when you called out after the train..." Her voice caught. "I thought it might be Him coming to take me to heaven."

"No, sweetheart," Josh whispered. "Not for a long time yet."

Before he could ask who else might be traveling with her, a light flickered through one of the broken windows overhead, turning the darkness in the passenger car to a shadowy gray.

A pair of childish arms came around his neck, clutching the wool collar of his coat for dear life. "I'm glad it was you calling out to me, Dr. McClain."

The light faded just as Josh wrapped his arms around Ginger, holding her close, not sure who was more comforted by the action, the child or himself. But time was of the essence. Who knew how long they had before flames overtook the railroad car, and there were others needing help. A lantern flickered above them again, brighter this time, flooding the railcar with shards of light.

Keeping one arm around the girl's slender shoulders, Josh cupped his free hand around his mouth. "We're here!"

The illumination grew, chasing the darkness away,

washed-out colors coming into focus until light shone just overhead like the midday sun on a cloudless day. A bearded man appeared in what once was a window. "Anybody in there?"

"Mr. Woods?" Ginger asked.

"Ginger!" The bedraggled man leaned in, reaching out his arms to the child. "We've got to get you out of there. Now."

The sense of urgency in the man's voice lifted the hairs on the back of Josh's neck. Pushing the child gently away from him, Josh met her worried eyes before glancing down at her arm. "I'm going to lift you up to Mr. Woods now, sweetheart, but it may hurt a little bit. Okay?"

"What about you?" Ginger's lower lip wobbled at the question.

"I'm not going to leave him behind, sweet girl," the man answered, a brief smile cutting through his massive whiskers. "Now, let's get you out of there."

Satisfied, Ginger nodded. Josh grasped her around her waist and lifted her up toward the light, watching as she disappeared through the window. With a quickness he didn't know he had, Josh hurried through the overturned car, looking for the conductor he'd been talking with when the crash had occurred. Suddenly, the floor beneath him rumbled, knocking him into the wall. Josh raised his hand and pressed it flat against the varnished wood, then snatched it back as heat radiated through his palm.

Fire!

"Spread out along the tracks," Dr. Katie Clark instructed the small band of college students, the twisted metal and smoldering wood from the train wreck casting ghostly shadows on the freshly fallen snow. "We don't want to miss any victims who might have been thrown free of the wreckage."

With a collective nod, the men and women fanned out, some holding their brand-new medical bags, though Katie knew most carried the bare essentials of a first-year student. The heavy blizzard that had blanketed the area for much of the early evening now formed a lacy curtain of white around them. Nearby, horses stamped nervously at the ground, while off in the distance tiny pinpoints of lantern light scattered through the streets as townspeople hurried toward the church to prepare for the injured patients.

Katie closed her eyes. *Help us, Lord. Help us help these people.*

A deep growl from nearby drew Katie's attention to the tree line a few yards from where the last car had come to a stop. It wasn't unusual for wolves to scout the woods outside of town, and the scent of fresh blood might draw them out in the open. She scanned the landscape, searching for man or beast.

Standing still, she called out, "Hello!"

She heard it again, a low strangled groan, off to her right. Checking the knotted rope that secured her medical bag around her waist, Katie lifted her lantern and waded toward the sound, her skirts and petticoats twisting into heavy, wet knots around her legs, the rope at her waist pulling against the deep drifts. Snow fell over the tops of her knee boots, her wool stockings no match for the clumps of ice puddling around her frozen toes. Katie gritted her teeth. When this was over, she'd convince Liberty Judd to make her a pair of wool pants, no matter how unconventional that might be!

Another groan drew Katie toward a padded bench with splintered wood sticking out at all angles, broken like seasoned twigs ready for the fireplace. As she moved closer, she noticed a pair of well-toned calves clad in leather boots sticking out from underneath. Katie planted the lantern beside her, then dropped down beside the man, taking his wrist in her hands, noting the strong heartbeat pulsing beneath her fingertips. "Sir, can you hear me?"

He grunted in response.

"Let me get this off of you." Katie grasped a broken slat and tugged, the wood making a loud pop when it finally released its grip. She repeated the action, the muscles in her shoulders starting to ache with each tug, every pull, until beads of sweat pooled around the gathers of her waist, leaving her wet and uncomfortable.

With the last broken piece, Katie grabbed the lantern and turned back toward the man, her eyes roaming over him in a quick assessment. No odd angles from either his arms or legs, which bode well. But she'd have to do a more thorough exam for any broken bones when they arrived at the church. There was no blood either except for a small cut under his right eye. His nose had been broken but not tonight, earlier, probably in his youth, but it did nothing to distract from the rugged angles that made his face strangely appealing.

"Are you an angel?"

Katie lifted her gaze, surprised to discover the man staring back at her. In the pale lantern light, silver threads shimmered around the edges of his blue-black eyes. There was something about the shape of his face, square with a dominant chin creased by a slight dimple, that seemed familiar to her. Probably just her mind playing tricks at this late hour.

She drew in a deep breath and held it for a moment, allowing the cold air to clear her head. Time to act like a physician, not some cow-eyed girl mooning over an attractive man. "You've been in a train wreck, Mr.…?"

"You didn't answer my question."

"What?"

"Are you an angel?"

The soft twang to his words reminded Katie of the warm summer days of her girlhood, before loss and grief had driven her and her father north to Michigan. She jerked at the rope around her waist until she could reach her medical bag and opened it, extracting a roll of bandages. "Considering all the angels mentioned in the Bible are male, I certainly hope not."

The low rumble of laughter in his throat caused a pleasant tremble in the pit of her stomach. "Are you certain about that?"

"Quite." Just what she needed tonight, a shameless flirt who was handsome to boot. Katie pulled her scissors out of her bag. "Maybe I should loan you my Bible while you're recuperating. You can catch up on your reading."

"I appreciate the gesture, but I have my own."

A Bible-toting charmer. The young ladies at the college would be all aflutter over this one. Who would be nursing a broken heart after this gentleman was on his way?

"You're very quiet."

"I'm examining you," she answered, a bit more sharply than she wanted to. Bending closer, she noticed a large patch of blue swelled across the apple of his right cheek. With the tenderest of touches, she rested her thumb against the crest of his cheekbone. "You have a large contusion on your cheek which worries me. May I check for broken bones?"

He nodded.

"This may hurt." Katie pressed her thumb against his cheekbone.

His lips pulled into a straight line, then relaxed as she released the pressure. "It's sore, like I've been punched in the face. But not broken."

Good, that meant less chance of something more serious, such as a brain injury. "Can you tell me where you hurt?"

"Quite a few places at the moment," he answered, a hint of sarcasm in the cracked tones of his voice. He cleared his throat, then spoke again. "Mostly bumps and bruises."

"Do you have a headache?"

"You ask a great many questions."

"I'm nosy." She smiled, patting her way down his left arm, feeling the hard muscles tense beneath the thick wool of his coat. "At least that's what my mother always said."

"Why? Did she catch you rifling through her belongings or something?"

"Worse," she answered, moving to his leg. "She found me reading my father's medical journals."

The man pushed himself up on his elbows and studied her. "Are you his nurse?"

Most people came to that conclusion when they discovered Katie assisted her father in his practice. She'd even considered going into nursing as a profession—there was no formal training, only what her father had taught her during her time as his assistant. But it hadn't been enough to satisfy her yearning to heal.

Katie shook her head, staring into her bag, anything to avoid his gaze. "I'm a doctor."

The man lay quiet as if digesting that piece of news while she continued her examination. Why should she think this man would be any different from the others who had talked her up, only to discover her profession and cower away from her as if she had the plague? The world needed female doctors; her papa had said so. But oddly enough, even that thought didn't take the sting out of this man's compounding silence.

Finally, he spoke. "My professor taught a very talented lady doctor. Elizabeth Blackwell."

"You've heard of Dr. Blackwell?"

He tried to smile, but ended up grimacing instead. "She was held up as an example during most of my schooling."

"She was honored at my graduation." Katie rocked back on her knees, a tiny flutter starting in her chest. "Where did you go to school?"

"University of South Carolina Medical School."

Katie's tongue felt thick against the roof of her mouth. "You're a doctor?"

He nodded. "Heading to Kansas to start a practice. And you?"

"Pennsylvania Medical College for Women." She thought it best to leave off the date of her graduation, seeing as it wasn't that long ago. She leaned forward to complete her assessment and found him studying her, his gaze tracing the line of her jaw before focusing his attention on her mouth. She drew back, a breath hitched in her lungs. Why did this man make her feel so off balance, so utterly feminine? "Do you remember anything about the accident?"

He tilted his head back, his gaze still trained on her. "The conductor said we were just outside of Hillsdale, said we'd be pulling into the station in a few minutes. Then the boxcar went sideways, like it skated down the tracks. It felt like forever before the car stopped tumbling once it flipped over." His throat convulsed in a swallow, his eyes wide. "How's Ginger?"

"Is that your wife?"

He shook his head. "No, she's a little girl who was in the same passenger car as me. We'd just managed to get her out when the fire started."

"We?"

"I didn't get a good look at the man who pulled Ginger out, but he was big, broad-shouldered, with hair spiked in different directions." He grimaced as she pressed a cotton square to his cheek.

"I'll look for her once we get everyone to the church. I know who Ginger is if she's from Hillsdale and not someone passing through. What does she look like?"

"It was too dark for me to get a good look at her, but she's almost nine. Tall for her age. Comes up to just below my chest."

The man looked so devastated, so discouraged, when all he had done was save this child's life. Wanting to comfort him, Katie reached out and laid her gloved hand on his shoulder. "I know who she is. We'll find her."

He lifted his hand as if to cover hers, then dropped it. "I'd appreciate that."

"How many passengers were in the car with you?" Katie asked, though she prayed not many. With the train running so late and the heavy snows, most travelers would have postponed their journey until daylight.

Only the most foolhardy would choose an uncomfortable bench seat over a hot meal and a warm bed.

So, what had driven this man to travel on such a night?

"Maybe a handful of people, including myself and Ginger, but I don't know what happened to them. It was so dark."

"Hopefully they managed to get out," she answered, turning to retrieve another cotton cloth to replace the dirty one.

The snow beside her shifted, the soft crunch drawing her attention back to her patient. The man had turned on his side, then, drawing his knees to his chest, he pushed up on his forearms until he could sit up.

"What do you think you're doing?" Katie asked.

"There are people around here who need help." A harsh hiss left his lips as he planted his palms on the ground to stand. Almost instinctively, he fisted his hands into his sides and crouched over.

Katie shot him the look she gave her father when he'd overdone. "And for the moment, you're one of them."

A tiny muscle in his jaw jerked. "Excuse me?"

If she hadn't taken the Hippocratic oath, she'd have wrung the man's stubborn neck. "You have a head wound, and while I don't think it's serious, you'll still need to be under observation for at least a few hours." She glanced down at his fists, then met his eyes with a seriousness she hoped he understood. "I don't know what kind of damage has been done to your hands yet."

"I'm fine," he answered with a sharp bite to his voice.

So he was stubborn, was he? Well, she could be just as mulish when she put her mind to it. Katie held out her opened hand, infusing iron in her voice. "Let me examine your hands."

He glanced down, his lips pulled in a tight line, equal parts pain and reluctance, then with a tentativeness that worried Katie, placed his fists in the palms of her hands. Scarlet borders traced an angry path across his wrist while a long opaque bubble of skin swelled across the fleshy pads of both thumbs. "How did you get burned?"

He caught his breath as she examined another blister, this one up the side of his pinkie finger. "A couple of men were trapped in the mail car in front of us. The fire got out of control. I couldn't reach them."

Empathy clogged Katie's throat. She knew what it felt like to try to save someone, only to lose them anyway. "I'm so sorry."

"Me, too." A note of weariness laced his words. This man may not have realized the extent of his injuries, but she did. The sooner Katie got him—well, all of the victims—out of the bitter cold and to the church, the better she'd feel.

"Dr. Clark? Can I do anything to help?"

Katie glanced up. Her father's friend Matthew Woods stomped through the snowdrifts toward them, his hunting bow tucked neatly behind his back. A fur trapper by trade, he must have been hunting the woods nearby when the trains collided. "I'd appreciate if you'd help this man to the church. And, please, tell my father I'll be there shortly. He'll be anxious to decide where all our patients will spend the night." Which would be unnecessary, Katie added silently, if the town council members would allow them to expand their practice and give her more responsibility.

"Your last name is Clark?"

Katie's attention shifted back to the man. Why was he so focused on her last name? She nodded. "Yes, Katie Clark."

"Short for Kathleen."

A sense of foreboding slid through her, as if caring for the train-wreck victims wouldn't be her greatest challenge in the coming days. However did this man know her Christian name, and more importantly, why?

"You don't remember me, do you, Katie Bug?"

Katie gasped. There was only one person who'd ever used that silly name for her—a boy, no more than eighteen the last time she'd seen him. That had been seven years ago, right after her mother had died. What was he doing here now, when she had finally forged a life for herself?

"Katie, are you okay? Who is this man?" Woody asked from his place beside her, concern lacing his voice.

"Let me introduce myself." The gentleness in his expression had taken on a hard edge as he glared at Katie before turning his attention back to Woody. "I'm Dr. Joshua McClain, Katie's fiancé."

Chapter 2

Josh watched the changing emotions on Katie's face, waiting for his words to finally sink in. Would there be tears? Anger? Or would her full pink lips turn up into a welcoming smile?

Instead, her mouth flattened into a sober line, her dark brown eyes studying his before glancing up at the man she called Woody. "He's taken a blow to the head, so he's a bit confused at the moment."

"I am not," he barked. "I'm as lucid as you are."

"You don't have to yell, young man." Woody glared at him, holding his shoulder in a steely grip. "Dr. Katie is only trying to help you."

Josh took a deep breath, then spoke. "I know, and I appreciate everything she's doing. But I'm not confused. We have been engaged for several years now."

She gasped, her head bowed low over her medical bag,

her hands not so steady as she shoved supplies back in the leather pouch. Was it possible she didn't know? From what he'd managed to get out of his father, Josh knew that Ethan Clark had been the one to come up with the idea of joining their two families through marriage, offering enough money to bail Josh's father out of his latest business mess, purchasing a husband for Katie in the process. As close as she'd always been to her father, she had to know of the agreement.

Didn't she?

Mr. Woods interrupted his thoughts. "Katie, your papa never told me you had an intended."

"That's because I don't, Woody." She threw the last of her instruments into her bag and slammed it shut. "Dr. McClain is confused."

"Doesn't sound all that confused to me." The older man's beard parted to reveal a wide smile. "Your papa will be tickled pink."

So Ethan Clark was looking to marry his daughter off, though why there'd be a problem, Josh wasn't quite sure. Even in the dim light of the lantern, he noticed Katie's creamy white skin, the light dusting of freckles across her nose, the dark brown hair threaded with strands of rich gold.

But it was her eyes that had captured his attention. Studious and sincere, they had always fascinated him in their youth, taking in everything as if she found the world around her the most incredible classroom.

The way she continued to stare at him right now, as if he'd grown a second head, made him wonder if Ethan Clark had bothered to tell his daughter of the agreement.

"Why have you waited so long to get married? I mean,

Katie here's been back from that medical college for going on a year."

Katie glared at the man. "We are not engaged."

Maybe Katie could help get them both out. Until he was assured the contract was null and void, he wouldn't be the only one suffering through this mess. Josh turned to Mr. Woods. "Dr. Clark thought it would be best if we gave Katie a little time to start her practice."

A strangled sound came from Katie, and he glanced over at her, finding her face had gone a deadly shade of white. Without thinking, he put his arm around her waist, her body swaying gently against him. Ethan Clark and his own father should be called out for causing Katie this kind of distress.

"You're the young man who saved little Miss Ginger!"

The girl from the train! "How is she?"

"Fine, fine. Ethan fit her with a sling for her shoulder, but I think it's more for show than anything else." Mr. Woods laughed, blind to Katie's discomfort, instead turning from one to the other, grinning like a puppy with two tails. "And now you're here to claim your bride. Just in time for Saint Valentine's Day, too!"

Josh shook his head. Who would have thought the old bear of a man would have a heart for the romantic? Not that it mattered. Once he got Katie to side with him on the absurdity of this marriage arrangement, he'd be on the first train out of town, heading to Kansas, to the new life God had blessed him with.

"Woody," Katie said, finally recovered, though her mouth was set in a painful flat line. Nothing like the full lips that had turned up at the corners he'd been admiring just a few minutes before. "Would you please take Dr. McClain over to our house and stay with him until

I get there? It shouldn't take too long once I give Papa's students their patient assignments."

Joshua blinked. Had the woman just dismissed him into the care of the old codger? No, God had called him to help the hurting, not sit in the background and watch. "As comfortable as I'm sure your home is, I'd rather help out."

Sitting back on her knees, Katie crossed her arms over her chest. "Then, pray tell, where is it that you'd like to go?"

"I take it you've set up a makeshift hospital?"

She nodded, her gaze suspect. One luminous strand of chestnut hair had pulled free of its confinement and blew in a soft wave against her cheek. "At the church."

"Then I can help." Josh brushed the palms of his hands against his pants leg, a million tiny straight pins shooting fire up his arm and across his shoulders. Cold air froze in his lungs, and for a second, the world around him blurred.

When his vision cleared, Kathleen glared at him like a disobedient schoolboy. "Your hands have been scalded. No."

The word grated on his nerves as it always did. "You don't know the magnitude of the injuries you'll face once you return to the church."

"And you're among those injured, Dr. McClain," she answered, rising to her feet gracefully, sodden snow and bits of grass clinging to her wrinkled skirts. "Until I do, you will remain a patient rather than a physician."

Blasted stubborn woman! He couldn't sit still, waiting on her to discharge him when there were people in need of a doctor. Was she going to let her pride get in the way of saving a person's life? "I'm an excellent surgeon."

"Not with those hands, you're not. Besides, both my father and I are prepared to operate if the need arises."

"There are a number of injured. Surely, you wouldn't deny them another doctor to work alongside you and your father," Josh said. At this point, even a simple task like fluffing pillows and serving coffee would be better than sitting back, wondering how he could have made a difference.

"How are you going to help them? Your eye is almost swollen shut. Your hands are not bad, but they're still slightly scalded." Her gaze dropped to the top button of his coat but not before he saw it, some glimmer of emotion that set his heart pulsing. "Please, just go back with Woody."

Josh grudgingly admitted to himself she was right. But he wasn't ready to concede the argument yet. "Can I at least wait at the church? That way, I'll be ready to work once you're satisfied I've been properly treated."

The muscles in her jaw tightened. "I don't…"

"You want me to hog-tie him for you, Katie?" Mr. Woods glared at him, his bushy gray eyebrows gathered in a taunt line over equally gray eyes. "I will, you know."

Josh could see the moment Katie gave up fighting him. "That won't be necessary, Woody." She repositioned her bonnet, then retied her ribbons. "Please, take him to the church. And make sure one of the students cleans his hands thoroughly and covers them with ointment."

"Yes, ma'am," Mr. Woods replied.

Old habits forged in childhood told Josh to thank her for relenting on this subject, but as he opened his mouth, Katie grabbed her wet skirts in one hand while balancing the lantern in the other and walked away.

"Just like a woman to up and leave when things get a bit interesting, eh?"

Josh narrowed his gaze on the old man beside him,

the pungent smell of animal hides clinging to him like a second skin. "I wouldn't know."

"Well, you'd better get used to it." The man snorted, taking Josh's arm and tugging him upward. "Especially if you're going to marry our Katie."

The icy ground shifted beneath Josh's feet as he stood. A strong arm settled around him, holding him up. Josh tilted his head to see Woods studying him. "There's nothing wrong with admitting you're hurt, son."

Ignoring the man, Josh planted his booted feet deeper into the snow. "You sound like you've known Katie for a long time."

The man hesitated for a moment, then nodded. "Since her papa moved into town some seven years ago. How about you?"

"We grew up together back in South Carolina." Two peas in a pod, his mother had called them, though an awkwardness sprang up between them the summer Katie began wearing her hair up, when her coltish form began to soften into womanly curves. The deaths of their mothers in a carriage crash had only deepened the ravine between them.

And now he was supposed to marry her.

"I've got to say, it's a little odd that Ethan never mentioned Katie being betrothed."

Probably too ashamed to admit how he'd taken advantage of the McClains, not that the loss of his mother absolved his father fully. "Like I said, Dr. Clark thought it best if Katie established herself in her profession a bit."

"That doesn't sound like Ethan. He's always been more partial to Katie making him a grandfather than becoming a partner in his practice."

Josh's gut tightened. If Clark was set on Katie marrying, breaking the marriage contract might prove to be difficult. He would have to figure out some way to convince the man to change his mind. A job waited for him out West, a chance to start the life God intended for him, and he couldn't afford to be saddled with a woman he hadn't seen in seven years.

"We're almost there," Woods said, pointing to a faintly lit area just in front of them where several horses stood, pawing the ground anxiously. Rows of bells tinkled softly from the leather harnesses connecting the animals to the sleighs. In contrast, the distant cries of the injured pierced the cold night air.

Josh steered his thoughts in a different direction. "Who were the students Katie spoke of?"

"Katie tutors some of the students over at the college, mainly her papa's anatomy class. But she's hoping to convince the president to let her teach." Woods smiled at him with paternal pride. "She's got an idea for training nurses through the college. Heard it from one of her friends who works in a ladies' hospital over in England."

"Sounds ambitious." A doctor and a professor. At least Katie would have something to fall back on when they dissolved this so-called engagement. But, he grudgingly confessed to himself, the woman must have gumption to take on such a grueling course. Not many ladies in his acquaintance could claim any sort of education past the expected handling of the household staff and needlework. Of course, most men wanted a woman like that, to be a helpmate, a heart to his head. Certainly not a colleague.

Who can find a virtuous woman? For her price is far above rubies.

The Proverb his mother had read to him many nights during their Bible reading pushed to the front of his thoughts. He'd always hoped for a love match, to find a young woman he could give his heart to, could share with, could grow with. Not the cold, clinical arrangement of a marriage contract.

"You know, like I said before, Valentine's Day is in a few days." Woody's statement startled Josh back to cold reality. "That's a pretty good day for a wedding, don't you think?"

"I'm sure Katie will need more time," Josh answered. He knew he did, at least until he could find the right woman to share his life, one who understood his desire to use his God-given gift of healing instead of being chained to his family's businesses in Charleston.

A golden hue of lamplight cast an eerie glow, creating long shadows of men placing makeshift stretchers on the sleighs playing out on a canvas of snowy-white. A woman stared at them, her eyes wide, dark holes swallowed up in the shadow of her pale face. A whimper of a lost child. Josh's gut twisted into a tight knot.

How can I help them, Lord?

If only he could convince the mountain man to help. "Woods, there are more people hurt than Katie and her father can manage."

"Maybe." The old man bent his head toward him, his gray bushy eyebrows high on his head. "You look like you've been in a brawl with an old grizzly and lost."

A slight smile tugged at Josh's lips. "Maybe, but what kind of doctor would I be if I didn't help?"

Woody seemed to consider that thought for a moment, then nodded. "Look, I'll help you once we get to the church, but take it slow. I don't want to have to explain this to Katie if you come up sick."

"Don't you worry. I'll take care of Katie."

Woods leveled a look at him, his bark of laughter echoing in the night air. "I believe you just might."

Katie walked behind the last of her father's students, swinging her lantern from side to side, studying the landscape, searching among the crushed snowdrifts that lined the tracks for hints of any remaining victims. Sleigh bells jingled softly as the last of the wounded were bundled up for the ride to the church along with two of the more advanced students who would monitor their condition. Maybe one day her own students would help in such efforts. Her lips curled up at the thought.

She rolled her shoulders back, trying to unknot the tight muscles frozen into place; her legs were numb beneath soaked layers of her petticoats and skirts. Locating and transporting the injured had gone better than she could have hoped given the conditions. Papa would be pleased.

Her gaze traveled past the last of the sleighs to the glowing outline of the town. Even from a mile away, she could just make out the pinpoints of light huddled around the white framed church, which would be the center of activity. Once she had a clearer idea of what they faced, she would prioritize, but in any event, she and her father had a long night ahead of them.

Even longer now because of Joshua McClain's arrival.

Kate grimaced, rubbing her hands together to stave off the tingling numbness in her fingers. Why, after all these years of silence, had he bothered to show up here in Hillsdale, claiming to be her fiancé? Her thoughts strayed, to a time when she was young and more carefree than now, when Josh was still her best friend and their mothers were still alive. Yes, things had become awkward between them, but they had been changing, growing up, and she had begun to notice Josh not as a childhood friend, but as a man.

Katie squashed the thought. More than likely, Josh was after money just like his papa. Well, he'd wasted his time. The Clarks had no funds, not counting the meager salary Papa drew for his dual role as town doctor and professor at the college. That barely covered their daily needs and restocked their medical supplies. She'd simply tell Joshua McClain the truth—the Clarks' fortune was gone. He probably wouldn't be able to buy a way out of town fast enough.

As she walked up to where the remaining sleighs sat parked, a tall man bustled toward her, the soberness of the situation doing nothing to take the starch out of his gait.

Ben Parker, mayor of Hillsdale and owner of Parker General store.

"Hello, Mayor," Katie said, stamping her feet, hoping to generate some blood flow in her numb legs.

"Miss Katie," he replied, tilting his head in a half acknowledgment. "Have you talked to your father yet about the conditions of the injured?"

Ben always did that, ignoring her professional title as if she were still a young girl buying a penny's worth of candy from him instead of medicines and medical journals. How was he and the rest of the town council going to react if her father followed through with his threats to retire from his practice and simply teach? Would that finally push them into accepting her as the town doctor?

She'd been prepared for Old Ben this time. Slipping her gloved hand in the front pocket of her cape, she extracted a scratch of paper and held it out to him. "I thought you might like some numbers, Mr. Mayor, but please, understand. These numbers are incomplete without my father's admissions."

"Do you have any idea when we might expect a full report on their conditions?"

Katie shook her head. "No, not really. I still need to get to the church and assess who needs surgery and who can wait. That's going to take time."

"But some of the uninjured passengers have been waiting over an hour for word about wounded family members."

Katie drew in a deep breath through her nostrils and slowly blew it out. She felt for the family members, truly she did, but she refused to be rushed, not at the cost of her patients' lives. "Ben, I'll have my assistant try to work up a report for you in the morning, but right now, I'm needed at the church."

Ben nodded, but the grim line of his mouth told her the mayor wasn't happy with her response. "I understand, Katie, and I know you're doing your best. Maybe you could ask your father to come find me when he has a moment?"

As if her father would have any more time to waste at the moment than she did. No wonder Papa had been threatening to quit medicine. Dealing with Ben's thickheadedness—well, the whole council's for that matter—must have been exhausting. Something for her to look forward to.

For the moment, she had other things on her mind. "Mr. Parker, we only have enough room to treat the most seriously injured at the church. So, if you could find some folks who might take in the rest of these people, I would appreciate it."

He nodded. "I'll arrange it and bring you a list shortly."

"Thank you."

Without acknowledging her, Ben turned and, with the same efficient pace, headed toward a group of men gathered around a campfire near the rails, long-necked rifles held tightly in their hands. Guards to watch the wreckage, she supposed. She could only pray there wouldn't be more patients later.

The ride into town went by quickly. Pushing through the crowd gathered outside the church, Katie wished she could give some kind of encouragement, anything to lift their spirits, but knowing the news could turn cruel, she remained silent as she slipped inside.

Katie immediately peeled off her gloves and cape, her fingers and toes tingling as the warmth of the room sank down into her frozen bones. Her booted feet clattered against the hardwood with each step, her bones so heavy, she couldn't help but wonder if her marrow had turned to ice. She clamped her eyes shut in a quick prayer. *Lord, give us the strength and wisdom we need to care for these people. Use our skills to help in any way we can.*

Looking out over the sanctuary, Katie could see her father's students had been hard at work. The pews had been shoved to either side of the church, leaving the center of the room open to accommodate one of the rectangular tables from Papa's anatomy lab. An uneven row of oil lanterns cast a steady stream of light around the room while candles of all shapes and sizes flickered closer to the center, where the unprotected flames would be shielded from the crosswinds. Quilts and blankets of faded blues, vivid oranges and butter-yellows carpeted the floor in pallets except for the cleared path the students used to get from one patient to the next.

"Dr. Clark."

Katie gave a half smile at the slender woman hurrying toward her. Ada Watkins had proved herself an excellent assistant in the past year, and a glowing example of what Katie hoped to accomplish training skilled nurses. “I’m so glad you’re here. We have our hands full tonight.”

Ada held out an apron for Katie, combing over a paper in her hands. “Most of our patients are settled in. I’ve made a list, numbering the injured in order of severity. I’ve also asked Pastor Quinn to round up all the spirits he can get his hands on, just in case the laudanum runs low.”

Katie slipped her arms through the apron’s openings, then turned, waiting for Ada to help her with the ribbons. “Good. I haven’t gotten this month’s supplies in yet, and a few bottles of spirits might come in handy.”

Ada tightened the strings around Katie’s waist and tied it off. “I figured it would be best if the pastor was the one explaining our need. Some people might not see the need to give up their spirits to just anyone.”

“Good thinking,” Katie agreed. Ada always used her head to think through a particular situation. It was what made her an exceptional assistant.

“This is going to hurt a bit, honey, but you’ll feel a lot better once we do it.”

Katie’s head jerked around at the sound of a soft familiar baritone. Less than three feet away, Josh McClain sat on the edge of a pew, tenderly cupping the elbow of a young girl in one large gloved hand while resting the other on her shoulder.

“Ready?”

Slamming her eyes shut, the child drew in a sharp breath and held it, then gave him a nod. Josh tugged, the muscles of his bare forearms tightening into corded sinew, disappearing beneath his pushed-up shirtsleeves.

He sucked in a breath, and for one brief moment, he looked ready to join in the child's plaintive cry.

He must have felt the shoulder slip back into place because he eased up, laying the girl's arm along her side before tucking the quilts under her chin. "You just rest now. Let that medicine we gave you help you sleep."

A halo of curls bobbed in response, then Katie watched the girl's breathing slow as she slid into a restful sleep.

Katie marched over and stood near the end of the child's pew, waiting, her temper melting any ice that had been running through her blood. When Josh finally stood and walked away, she followed him across the room to a table that had been set up with a stack of towels, a cake of Ursula's homemade soap, basins and pitchers of water for washing. "I would like a word with you, please."

"What can I do for you?" Snatching a fresh towel from the pile, he turned, and she got her first real look at his injuries. His right eye was swollen shut now, the cut across his right cheek gaping open. There was a large smudge of blood on his shoulder, whether his or someone he'd treated she couldn't be sure. His hands were gloved, but there was no denying the pained expression on his face as he continued to rub his covered hands against the towel.

"You need to stop treating patients. Now."

"I hope you don't mind how I arranged our little makeshift hospital," Josh answered, ignoring her request, his mouth drawn into a strained line, slight lines of pain deepening around his mouth and eyes with every movement of his hands. "Your students seemed a bit confused about how to proceed when I arrived."

The tiny spark of pride Katie had felt in her instructions faded with his words. She had expected too much from them, but at least Josh was here to lend his experience, not that she would ever tell him. She straightened. "We agreed you wouldn't treat patients until your injuries had been examined and tended to."

"I never agreed to that." Josh threw the towel into a growing pile of dirty linen, then turned to face her. He was much taller than she remembered, his fist planted on his hip. "You just dismissed me into Woods's care, and thought I would do whatever you commanded without a second thought."

Anger and common sense warred inside her until sensibility won out. No use arguing with the man; it would only upset him more. And her papa had always said you could catch more flies with honey than with vinegar. Holding out her upturned palms, Katie glanced down at his gloved hands. "May I?"

He eyed her with an air of suspicion. "What are you going to do?"

For a moment, he reminded her of the boy he used to be, his head tilted slightly, his straw-colored hair mussed from hours of play. They'd been so close once, the best of friends until maturity and awareness set in. An awareness she felt even now. She swallowed at the thought. "I just figured that if I see to your wounds, we could agree whether it's a good idea for you to continue working or not. Do you agree?"

Her change in tactic seemed to puzzle him. "But there are some severe injuries...."

"They're being tended to, I can assure you," she said, stretching up on tiptoe to assess his pupils but instead sinking into deep fathoms of blue. She must be more tired than she thought. She lowered herself back to the ground. "The only way I will consider allowing you to assist is if I clear you to help. Understand?"

"I guess," he answered grudgingly.

"Good. Let's get you fixed up." Katie cupped his elbow, suddenly aware of the warm skin, taut muscles beneath her fingertips. When had she turned back into a silly little schoolgirl? Despite her chiding him, her knees felt wobbly as she led him to a blanket-covered pew and watched him sink down onto it. "Excuse me while I get some supplies and talk to my assistant for a moment."

"My hands aren't that bad, you know. Just scalding, I think." Josh experimentally stretched his gloved hands out, the color in the unbruised parts of his face suddenly pale.

Please, God, don't let him be going into shock. Katie grabbed a quilt from the back of the pew and spread it over him. "Here, wrap up in this. We need to get you warmed up."

Josh shook his head, trying to push the blanket away. "I don't need that."

Still as obstinate as ever. "Just for a few minutes," she murmured, tucking in the ends, noticing how broad his shoulders had become in the seven years since she'd last seen him. "You were out there in the cold for a long time."

"So were you." His familiar crooked smile made her heart flutter. "I'm willing to share, you know."

Heat rose up her neck and burst into her cheeks. Josh had always been a tease, ready with a quick wit just to get a rise out of her, to shock her serious sensibilities. It was one of the things she'd always loved about him. Well, two could play at that game. "What if I took you up on that? What then?"

One dark brow lifted. "Not as easily ruffled as you used to be, I see."

"Training to be a doctor can do that to a person."

"Still, it took a lot to unsettle you even as a little girl," Josh said, all traces of playfulness gone from his voice. "I enjoyed making you blush."

"And you were such an expert at it." Katie gave him a slight nod. Was that what was behind this whole engagement business he'd told Woody about at the wreckage? Was it just a childish joke between old friends? A faint sense of disappointment drifted through her. Josh wouldn't be that cruel, would he? "Let me find my assistant and get the supplies I need to work on your hands."

He didn't answer, but nodded.

Katie gave him one last look over, then, satisfied, she turned, only to find her assistant standing a few steps away as if waiting for instructions. She hurried over to her. "I was just coming to find you. How is everything going?"

"Very good, actually. Most of the injuries are turning out to be less severe than first thought."

Thank You, Lord!

Ada's gaze shifted to the pew where Josh sat, and she smiled. "I see you've found Dr. McClain. Handsome fellow, even with the black eye."

Katie's chest tightened. Jealousy? She didn't even know the man, just the boy he'd been. "I guess, if you like that type."

Ada chuckled softly. "He seems to be a very determined man, just the sort who could handle an equally determined woman. Say, a lady doctor?"

Oh, dear. "Really, Ada. Don't we have enough on our hands at the moment without your playing matchmaker?"

"I guess so."

Katie took a deep breath to steady herself. "Anyway, have you seen my father?"

Her assistant nodded. "He arranged for the most serious cases to be moved to your offices. Thought it would be best not to have an audience during surgery."

Made sense, though she wondered how she would manage seeing patients here and assisting her father. Maybe Mr. Rothchild or one of the other more advanced students could be left in charge. "When did he want to get started?"

"I believe he already has. He sent for Mr. Rothchild and Mr. Anderson a little while ago."

Disappointment slid through her. Why couldn't his students stitch cuts and set bones while she worked alongside her father? Didn't Papa understand the message it sent to the town council, the people of Hillsdale? That he didn't have confidence in her abilities?

But there was no fighting his decision now. "Ada, I need to stitch up Dr. McClain's cut." She gave the young woman a list of supplies she needed. "Oh, and a cup of strong coffee with plenty of sugar and cream with twenty drops of laudanum, please?"

Ada gave her a skeptical look. "You think sugar and cream will mask the bitter taste?"

"Probably not. But the burns on his hands need to be examined, and that cut below his eye is very deep." She stretched her neck. "I need him to be very still if I'm going to stitch it properly."

"Think it's going to leave a scar?"

"More than likely. But the ladies won't mind. In fact, they'll probably be even more drawn to him, wanting to know how he came to acquire his mysterious scar." Katie frowned at the thought. "Maybe we should use an ice pack on his eye. That should help reduce the swelling so he doesn't scar as badly."

"Yes, Doctor." Ada gave her a knowing smile, then hurried away.

Chapter 3

Josh leaned back against the pew and closed his good eye, letting his head roll back against the blanketed wood, the moans from around the room a soothing melody that lulled him. Oddly enough, the hint of carbolic acid, lye soap and lavender that drifted in the air comforted him, and he dug deeper into the quilts. There weren't as many injured as he'd thought. A good thing, he decided. He hadn't known until Katie had forced him to sit down just how bad he felt.

A nest of bees seemed to have taken up residence on his hands, piercing the tender flesh of his palms over and over, a venous heat running up the insides of his arms. Josh flexed his fingers, trying to get away from the constant stinging, but the pain only multiplied and he let out a grunt.

"Josh?" A warm hand rested on his shoulder, long

tapered fingers that stirred new sensations that went straight to his heart. He forced his eye open and found Katie standing in front of him, her chocolate-brown eyes brimming with worry.

He straightened, though the simple action caused his bones and muscles to hum in a high-pitched ache, another groan threatening on his lips. The pain finally dulled, and he nodded, not yet trusting his voice.

"I think the day has finally caught up with you," Katie said quietly, sinking down beside him, her gaze assessing. "Here, let me help you with this."

She unfolded one of the cotton towels and draped it loosely over his shoulders, her face little more than an inch from his as she fussed with the ends. Her skin looked as soft as velvet, creamy except for the pale brown freckles across the bridge of her nose. Her mother had always forced her to wash her face in lemon juice, hoping to bleach those delicate specks. Josh smiled. Thank goodness, she hadn't succeeded.

"Here, this should make you feel better." Katie lifted a steaming mug to Josh's lips. "But be careful. It's hot."

"I've never heard of anyone prescribing coffee before."

Her lips darted up in a quick smile. "Maybe I should have one of my father's students write a study on it. The effects of coffee as a pain reliever and mood enhancer."

Josh took a sip, the combination of bitter and sweet leaving him with an awful taste in his mouth. Had she laced the stuff with laudanum to dull the pain? The Katie he remembered wasn't that devious. No, she would have argued with him, giving him the merits of dosing him while he disagreed. Now he'd be alert and ready to discuss the agreement that had brought him here in the first place. "I might have to read that paper."

She gave him another sip. "You did a very good job getting everything organized around here. Thank you."

"You're welcome." For some odd reason, Katie's opinion mattered to him, though he couldn't understand why. She was surprisingly different than he expected, nothing like the bored debutantes back in Charleston who had an eye on marrying him for the family name. But Katie had always been different, going her own way when others stayed on the same course as the generations before them. Probably one of the reasons he'd always liked her so much. Her idea to train nurses was innovative, maybe even groundbreaking. If he hadn't already accepted a post in Kansas, he'd have planned to stick around for a few more days and get to know her again.

But how did one court one's own fiancée?

Josh swallowed the unexpected chuckle that bubbled in his throat. He glanced at the empty mug, then back at Katie. "You dosed me with laudanum, didn't you?"

"Just a little. I didn't want to have to argue with you for the next thirty minutes." She dropped a cloth into a basin filled with water, then picked it up and wrung it out. "Wouldn't you have done the same thing?"

His breath hissed out between his clenched teeth when she lifted the rag to his swollen eye. "Probably."

"I never would have expected you to agree with me so quickly." The smile in her voice caused something warm to unwind in him. Friendship? Maybe, but nothing like any friend he'd ever had before, except for Katie.

"Don't get used to it." Josh took a deep breath, his muscles uncoiling as the pain became a dull sting his senses were numbly aware of. Katie worked quickly, yet her gentle strokes comforted him, and he found it growing more difficult to keep his eyes open. "You're an excellent doctor, Katie."

Her slender fingers stilled. "I am?"

His head felt fuzzy, his thoughts disjointed, but he'd have to be a fool not to see Katie's accomplishments. Josh forced his eyes open. "And if your father's students are anything to go by, you've been a great help in educating the next generation of doctors."

"Thank you." Katie lowered her gaze then, the dark brown lashes floating down until they caressed the gentle swell of her cheek.

Josh swallowed. Would her skin be soft like the rose petals that grew in the sunny spot outside his window back home? He clenched his fingers into a ball and flinched. Must be the shock of the night and the pain making him think such foolishness.

"Did that hurt?"

"No," he slurred, surprised to realize that it was the truth. Katie tucked the edge of the cloth into his shirt collar, her fingertips brushing against his neck in gentle, warm movements. He leaned back, his muscles relaxing more with each breath. "I should have known you'd become a doctor. You were always fussing over every sick dog in Abbeville."

"Don't forget the cats. Remember that calico?"

He smiled at the laughter in her voice. This was the Katie he remembered, kind and funny, before time and the advent of their teen years had made interactions between them strained. She had been his dearest friend from his earliest memories. Then their mothers had died, and Katie had left before he could discover if she could be something more than a friend.

Josh hissed as Katie pressed a cotton square to his

cheek. "Sorry about that, but I want to get all the dirt out of the wound."

"I understand." He drew in a breath and held it, releasing it only after she moved away. "I'm sorry I made such a fuss before."

"I wasn't much better, barking at you when all you were doing was trying to help. And you just in a train wreck." Her lips tilted up in a small smile, and Josh couldn't help wondering if her mouth was as soft and sweet as it looked. "Mama would have boxed my ears if she were still alive."

"Still, you were the doctor in charge."

Katie didn't speak for a moment, and he wondered if she'd wandered away. But when she spoke, her breath warmed his face, the delicate scent of lavender teasing his nose. "Thank you, Josh. But know that I would have done the same thing that you did if our situations had been reversed."

He could see that, though he hated to think of Katie injured, well, anybody injured. His body felt heavy, his muscles loose. A drugged sleep threatened to overwhelm him, and he jerked. He was here for a reason, to break the marriage agreement so he could follow God's plan west. "Katie, about what I said when you and Woods found me this evening."

"Relax." Katie's hand cupped his jaw, making light circles under his ear, comforting him just as she'd done the day of the carriage accident, the day her mother passed away. "We can talk about it later."

He nodded, sleep dragging him further into the warm cocoon of his blankets. He heard a snip, felt the tight leather around his right hand and fingers loosen, but he was beyond caring.

* * *

Katie tied off the last stitch, then clipped the cotton fiber with her scissors. The snowy-white thread crisscrossed in neat rows against the purplish-blue gash on the woman's arm. She glanced up and smiled. "I'll need to change your dressings for the next few days, and you'll feel a bit sore. But I think you can be dismissed to your husband's care, Mrs. Alexander."

"Really?" The gray-haired woman looked at her through tired blue eyes. "I thought the doctor would want to check me first."

Katie had to hold back an exhausted sigh. It had been the same way all night, folks mistaking her for a college student or, at most, an assistant rather than a trained physician. At first, she'd just ignored it, but as the hours had worn on, she'd found herself biting her tongue to keep from making a bad situation even worse.

I'm sorry, Lord. These people have been through so much and here my pride is pricked. Help me see past my own need and find ways to help them. Katie picked up a long strip of linen and wound it comfortably around the woman's beefy arm. "My father is in surgery at the moment, but if it will make you feel any better, I've worked with him for quite some time."

The dubious look in the lady's expression told Katie she didn't believe her. Mrs. Alexander patted her hand. "I'm sure you're very good with a needle, dear. Most women have to be to keep up with the mending and the sewing that needs to be done around the house. Why, Mr. Alexander alone could keep me busy for a month."

Katie simply nodded. She had run out of words trying to convince people they were in good hands. Only Josh had believed in her abilities.

"I certainly do appreciate all the work you've done helping all of us from the wreck, but I'm betting your husband probably wishes you were home," the older woman said, tugging her torn sleeve down gently, careful not to upset her dressings. "Probably has his hands full with your little ones."

Katie rolled up the leftover cloth before tucking the loose edge gently inside, a small knot of longing tangling deep in her chest. Why was this woman's chatter about a husband, home and children bothering her so badly? She'd accepted her fate, understood her profession would scare off any man she might take an interest in. Truth be told, there had been only one, and he hadn't known she existed, at least not in the romantic sense.

Her gaze slid across the room to where Josh lay. She and Ada had managed to maneuver his strapping bulk onto the pew, though just barely, her fingers tingling at the memory of his muscular shoulders and the long length of well-proportioned legs encased in dark trousers and black boots that dangled to the floor. He'd been rakishly handsome at sixteen, but now it was more than that. There was a sturdiness about him, a confidence that only came with age and experience. Katie's heart fluttered. All the girls in South Carolina must be mourning his loss.

But why had he come to Hillsdale? What had led him to think they were engaged?

"Do you think that's the young man who saved the little girl from the fire in the postal car?" Mrs. Alexander asked, looking over Katie's shoulder to where Josh lay.

"I don't know," Katie answered, still watching him, unconsciously counting his slow, even breaths. In the hours after the wreck, stories of bravery began spreading around the sanctuary, but nothing compared to Ginger

Livingston's tale of the man who had found her huddling in darkness and lifted her out of the train car just as it burst into flames. Katie had put two and two together instantly, but thought it best to wait until Josh was awake to confirm it.

"The man who did that is nothing short of a hero in my book, putting himself in harm's way for the sake of that child." The older woman lifted her reticule and opened it, extracting a few coins. "The Southern Michigan ought to give him a medal for what he did."

Katie nodded. The Josh she knew would hate all the notoriety of being hailed a hero. But what about this Josh, the man he'd become? Just from his actions tonight, his need to help despite his own injuries, she'd guess he'd still find being thought of as a hero uncomfortable.

"How much do I owe you?"

"Nothing," Katie answered. Dr. Etheridge had sent word from her father that they would wait and settle up with the railroad for all the passengers' treatments, though why Papa thought the Southern Michigan would pay was beyond her.

"That's mighty kind of you, Miss Katie. Mighty kind."

Katie didn't want to think of what this kindness may cost her, especially when she had to decide between restocking medical supplies or buying food next month. Maybe the railroad would come through and pay them. If not, God would provide.

A tall, wiry man with white tufts of hair along the sides of his head and face hurried toward them. "Has Miss Katie about finished up with you, my dear?"

Katie couldn't help but smile. Thomas Alexander was another hero of the train wreck, having helped Dr. Etheridge draw up a list of the passengers then matching them to families in Hillsdale who had opened their homes. Friendly and confident, he reminded Katie of her papa in the old days, before the accident had taken her mother and their lives had swirled out of control. "She's all ready."

"That's lovely." Mr. Alexander lifted his wife's hand gently, his eyes only on her. "And you're sure you're all right, dearest?"

"Yes." The older woman's cheeks bloomed with a light blush, turning back the clock, acting for all the world as a young girl with her first beau.

Katie lowered her gaze to her lap. It was sweet, really, this devotion between the Alexanders. And, she admitted to herself, it hurt to think she'd never have that for herself. But she'd put any romantic expectations behind her when God had opened the doors for her to go to medical school. Healing the sick was God's plan for her life. Even knowing that, she couldn't deny wanting a home, children and a husband who loved her for herself.

No sense mooning over what she'd never have. Katie briefly went over instructions with the Alexanders, noting on a scratch piece of paper that they would be at Ursula's boardinghouse if a house call was needed.

As the couple left arm in arm, Ada walked slowly toward her, her apron wrinkled and stained, strands of brownish-blond hair hanging in strings around her pale face. "They're a nice couple, aren't they?"

"Yes, they are." Katie stretched her arms over her head and leaned to one side. "So, who's next?"

"No one. We're through."

"Really?" Katie grabbed the edge of her apron and wiped her hands. "Are you sure?"

"Everyone's been treated and released." Her assistant poked a thumb in Josh's direction. "Except for the slumbering giant over there. He's been out for a couple of hours now."

"I'm glad. He didn't need to be up, running around, taking care of people, making that eye swell up even more."

"What about his hands?"

"Not as bad as I'd thought. Give him a day or two and he'll be back bothering me to see patients." Katie glanced at Josh's bandaged hands. The burns had been far less than she'd expected, sensitive from a blast of steam with two small blisters that she'd have to keep an eye on. But it could have been so much worse, and for that, she'd lifted up a prayer of praise.

"Poor soul." Ada chuckled. "He looked more like a prizefighter than a physician when he first came in, with that swollen eye and everything."

"Oh, don't let his title fool you. He once brought down a man nearly twice his size with one punch, just to protect a little girl and a feeble old dog," Katie replied. She'd been barely fourteen, hunched over that old bluetick hound, but she'd never forgotten how certain she'd been that Josh would protect her. It was the day she'd fallen in love with him.

"Sounds like a good man," Ada said on a yawn.

"Oh, Ada, go home and get some rest."

The woman glanced around. "But the mess…"

"I'll clean up as much as I can, then leave the rest until we have some help moving things back into place."

"And Dr. McClain?"

"I'll have to talk to Dr. Etheridge about placing him with a family," Katie answered, though she didn't like the idea. Josh's wounds might not be as severe as she'd first thought, but blisters could still turn septic, and a doctor's lifeblood was his hands.

Ada shook her head. "Mr. and Mrs. Alexander took the last space available. And the boardinghouse is busting at the seams with all the students and train passengers staying there."

There was only one place left. "Then I guess he'll just have to stay with us."

Ada moved in closer, her voice dropping though there was no one around to hear them. "Do you think that's proper? I mean, it's all over town that he told Mr. Woods you were his fiancée."

Katie checked her watch pinned to her bodice. "Five hours. That has to be a new record."

"Oh, don't get your dander up. It's just that Dr. McClain is something of a hero, and with you two being betrothed…" Ada gave her a silly smile. "It's kind of romantic."

The woman must be addle-brained from lack of sleep. "Ada, Dr. McClain withstood a traumatic event last night, and though his injuries weren't serious, he did receive a blow to the head which seems to have muddled his thinking at that moment."

"So, you're not getting married?"

The woman looked almost as distressed as Katie felt. She shook her head. "No."

"Too bad. You two seemed to get along quite well when you were treating him." Ada gave a brief shrug of her shoulder, then turned and walked away.

Katie took a deep breath, then leaned her head forward, stretching her neck. Explaining that her "engagement" to Josh had been a figment of his imagination was going to be a mess she'd have to clean up once he was safely out of town. Until then, she just hoped no one would mention it.

"You don't know."

Katie jerked her head up, turning to find Josh staring at her, the blankets gathering around his feet as they slid down his torso and legs when he sat up. "Well, good morning. We were wondering if you were going to sleep in today."

He stared at her, his expression a mixture of deep concern and disbelief. "You don't know, do you?"

An uncomfortable knot formed in the pit of Katie's stomach. "About what?"

Josh stood, wobbling a bit as he glanced around. "Where is everybody?"

"We just released our last patient. I thought I'd straighten up a little before I woke you." Katie felt herself go warm at the intimacy of the statement.

"You dosed me with laudanum." He put his hand to his forehead, then winced. "Why'd you do that?"

Katie took a measured step forward. "I had to take care of your hands, and there was no way you were going to sit still enough for me to suture that cut right below your eye. Don't you remember me explaining this all to you last night?"

He nodded slightly. "Vaguely. I just hate I wasn't able to help."

Josh still hadn't answered her question. "What did you mean when you said I didn't know something? What were you talking about?"

He stared at her, his expression some emotion she couldn't quite put her finger on. "You told that woman we weren't engaged."

Oh, dear. Maybe the man did have a concussion. He'd

have to have one if he thought they were engaged. Katie stepped closer, checking his eyes, trying to decide if his pupils were equal in size. She lifted her hand to gently pry open his swollen eye. "Do you have a headache or feel queasy?"

Quick as a bird, Josh caught her wrist in his wrapped hand, the warmth of his covered fingers circling her skin in a loose bracelet. "I don't have a concussion, Katie."

"Then what are you talking about?" She swallowed. "Why does it bother you so much that I told Ada we aren't engaged?"

"Because we are."

Katie felt as if all the air had been sucked out of her lungs. "I don't understand."

He dropped her hand then, stuffing his fist into his pocket, almost as if he couldn't bear the thought of touching her. "Your father coerced mine into signing a marriage contract. Your dowry for a husband, signed, sealed and delivered."

Chapter 4

"That's almost medieval."

Of all the things Josh had imagined Katie saying about the marriage contract, this was the least likely response. But then, he'd been going on the assumption that she had somehow wiled her way into the negotiations. Why he thought Katie capable of masterminding this entire mess, he wasn't sure, only it seemed like something any number of ladies would do for the opportunity to bear the McClain name. Why should she be any different?

But she was, he'd already decided. Very different from any lady he'd ever known.

"Yes, it is," he said, following Katie as she walked to the washing table and began rinsing her hands. "But our fathers drew it up nevertheless."

She grabbed a bar of soap and scrubbed it between her palms, translucent bubbles forming between her fingers and over her knuckles, a faint line forming between her brows. "I don't understand. How could Papa agree to such a thing without telling me?"

The disappointment in her voice caused a deep pain near his heart. She'd always been closer to her father than he could ever be to Samuel McClain. Ethan Clark had wounded her, deeper than any physical injury could touch. The man had broken his daughter's heart.

Somber brown eyes stared up at him. "You said my father coerced yours into signing this agreement. Why do you say that?"

"After the carriage accident, my father ran through quite a lot of money, paying doctors and such. He even put our home up for collateral at the bank." Josh hesitated for a moment. "Anything to help restore Mother's health."

"But she died anyway," Katie whispered. "Just like Mama."

Josh nodded. "Father went a little mad after that, drinking and wondering what might have been if Mother had lived. That's when your father approached him with the idea of a marriage contract."

Katie looked down at her soapy hands, glancing around as if unsure what to do next. Reaching for the water pitcher, Josh struggled to wrap his bandaged hand around the handle. He lifted it slightly, just enough to tilt the contents of the jug over her hands.

"Thank you." She took the pitcher from him and set it down on the table, then grabbed a clean towel to dry her hands. "Why would my father do something like that?"

"I always figured it was to purchase you a husband, but that was when I thought you..." Josh stopped, realizing as he spoke that his assumptions hadn't been too kind to Katie.

She must have realized it, too, because she balled up the towel and threw it at his head. "You conceited, arrogant..." She halted then, pressing her lips together in a tight line. "Rest assured, Dr. McClain, I did not suggest such a harebrained scheme to my father. Where would you get such a nonsensical idea?"

Nonsensical! "I'm very sought after among the ladies in Charleston."

"Really? And what was it they found so attractive about you? Your overinflated opinion of yourself? Or your egotistical manner?"

Josh gawked at her. When had he decided Katie had to be behind the marriage arrangement? Or had it just been wishful thinking, the way he'd thought of declaring himself to her all those years ago, when his friends began noticing her that summer before their mothers had died? What he'd give to take Katie's delicate hands in his and confess what a sorry mess he'd made of this whole situation. But he wasn't sure if she was ready to hear the rest of the story, not when the blue smudges under her eyes seemed to grow darker with each moment, and she looked ready to fall into a heap on the floor.

Instead, he leaned down and picked up the towel, tossing it on the table. "It's time to get you home."

Katie seemed to deflate in front of him. "I hate when you do that."

"What?" Gently, he turned her, reaching for the ties of her apron, tugging one cotton cord until the knot slipped open.

Shucking off the soiled smock, Katie tossed it to the side. "Think you're protecting me when actually you're keeping something from me."

"I just thought..."

She held up her hand. "You're probably right. What I need right now is some food and a little sleep. But when I wake up, I want to hear the rest of it, all right?"

"All right."

The next few minutes were spent doing menial tasks: banking the fire, gathering and folding blankets, piling up the dirty linens. When Katie was satisfied, they walked in silence to the vestibule to gather their things.

As Katie secured the church door, Josh glanced around. The world seemed devoid of color. Grayish skies hung low enough to touch the thick snowy-white blanket that carpeted the ground. The crisp fresh air chased away the memories of blood and sweat that had penetrated his dreams during the long night. The wind whistled mournfully, drowning out every other sound.

"Guess everyone is still in bed after last night," Katie said, breaking the silence.

"Maybe they're staying indoors because of the snow."

Katie chuckled softly, her fingers working the satin ribbons of her bonnet into a neat knot. "If that was true, we'd never get anything accomplished, seeing how it snows quite a bit of the time here."

"Do you like it here?" He held out his arm for her.

"It was hard at first, probably because leaving Abbeville meant facing the fact that Mama was really gone." She threaded her arm through his, resting her hand on his forearm. "It wasn't until I left for college that I really came to appreciate what I had here. Somewhere along the way, Hillsdale had become my home."

Josh nodded. Would he ever think of Kansas as his home? It seemed unlikely. But glancing down the street, he could understand why Katie had fallen in love with this place. The quaint clapboard houses and little shops that lined the sidewalk felt homey, considerate, just like the people who'd come to the aid of the victims last night. A rare find these days, when there seemed to be talk of war in every conversation back in Abbeville.

The muted crunch of snow under their boots echoed softly as they walked down the sidewalk toward the center of town. Josh felt Katie slip once or twice and grasped her waist to steady her, glancing at her as she forced her eyes open. Poor dear, she was dead on her feet. If he knew where she lived, he might be tempted to pick her up in his arms and carry her the rest of the way, but as that wasn't an option, he needed to keep her awake.

"What made you decide to go into medicine?"

Katie tilted her head back, her eyes taking a moment to focus on him. "Trying to keep me awake, hmm?"

"Yes, but I'm interested in knowing the answer, too."

She leaned her head against his arm, her hand curving around his biceps, her warmth radiating through the thick wool of his coat. "I figured you'd wonder why a woman would choose to study for a profession at all."

"Why wouldn't they?" Josh studied her, wishing the narrow brim of her bonnet did more to shield Katie from the elements.

She yawned. "Because we're expected to marry and have children, not take up a profession."

"But lots of women choose not to marry."

"Or love someone who doesn't love her back." Her voice wavered slightly.

Was that what had happened to Katie? Had she given her heart to a man, only to have it tossed back at her? Fool, he thought, tightening his grip on her waist. Anyone with a brain in his head would have noticed the kind of woman Katie was. Why, he hadn't been around her in over seven years and could see in an instant that she'd make the perfect wife.

The thought stole his breath. Just not for him.

"Our house is right up here, to the right."

The little gray house was smaller than Josh would have imagined, considering Dr. Clark performed surgeries and he and Katie saw patients there. But there was a homeyness about it, with its white lace curtains hanging in the front windows and the plume of smoke coming from the stone chimney that promised a roaring fire. As they walked up the path to the front door, Josh noticed a hand-carved sign.

Ethan Clark, M.D.

"Why isn't your name up there alongside your father's?"

Before Katie could answer him, the front door flew open, and a young woman barreled toward them, her cape hanging down behind her as if thrown on in a hurry. Josh tightened his hold on Katie, bringing her flush to his side as he held his free hand out. "Excuse me."

"Oh," the woman said, startled, pressing her hand to her chest. "You scared me."

"Ada?" Katie asked. "What are you doing here?"

"I was just coming to get you."

Katie shrugged out of his arms and straightened. "Is something wrong?"

"It's your father," Ada answered, her wide-eyed fear making Josh uneasy. "He's been stabbed!"

The next few moments passed in a terrifying blur as they hurried into the front hall. Katie fumbled with the small button of her cape until finally Josh pushed her hands away and helped her, making short work of the buttons even with his bandaged hands.

"Tell us what happened," Josh instructed.

"I don't rightly know. I was having a cup of coffee with Mrs. Holden when Ben Parker barged into the kitchen. Said that there'd been a problem down at the jail and that your father had been stabbed. A few minutes later, Sheriff Dawes pulled up in front of the house and a group of men carried the doctor upstairs. Mr. Rothchild and Mr. Anderson are with him now."

"What does the wound look like?" Katie asked, hoping against hope it wasn't as bad as Ada had made it out.

"A deep cut to his thigh."

Kate couldn't feel, her heart numb as her mind sped through an array of possibilities, each one worse than the last. If the blade nicked the artery… No, she couldn't think of that, not yet, not until she assessed the situation herself.

Josh's firm fingers tightened around her elbow, steadying her as her control threatened to slip away. "I'm here, Katie Bug."

"I couldn't bear it if he…" She choked on the last word.

Josh reached up and pulled the ribbons on her bonnet and gently lifted it from her head. "Let's wait until we have all the facts before we get too worried, okay?"

Katie nodded, sniffing back tears. Josh was right. Until she did an examination, she wouldn't know what kind of damage had been done.

"Lord, please calm Katie's fears. Please give her a peace that passes all understanding."

Katie glanced up at Josh, his head bowed over hers, his lips moving in quiet prayer. No one except her parents had ever prayed over her before. That Josh would, after all this time apart, touched her more than any words she could express. Instead, she lowered her head and joined him. *And, Lord, if this is Papa's time, give me the strength to go on by myself, trusting in You.*

She lifted her head and found Josh watching her. "Are you ready now?"

Katie nodded. "Ada, did they put Papa in his room?"

"Yes," the woman answered, suddenly looking anxious. "I hope that was all right."

"Of course." Katie reached out and squeezed her nurse's hand. "Papa will be more comfortable in his own bed. Thank you for being here."

Ada's cheeks turned pink. "You know I'd do anything I could for you and your father."

"I know."

Josh's hand settled against her lower back, comforting, steady. "Are you ready, Katie?"

She hesitated for a brief moment, then nodded, corralling her sodden skirts into her fists. Maybe his wounds wouldn't be as bad as all that, maybe just a cut she could practice her suturing skills on. Or maybe Papa had already bled out, died, and no one had wanted to tell her.

"Breathe, dearest," Josh whispered against her ear. "I'm here if you need me, remember?"

"Yes." This was Josh, her Josh. Her childhood friend, the boy who'd soothed her tears when Mama had died. The only man she'd ever loved. For the briefest of moments, Katie yearned to lean back against his solid chest, ask him to wrap his arms around her, cocoon her in his unwavering strength.

She made it up the stairs somehow, focusing her thoughts on her father and what supplies they might need if surgery was necessary.

"Kathleen." Randolph Dawes, the town's sheriff, came lumbering toward them. As he drew near, he bowed his head slightly, touching the rim of his felt hat.

"Rand, I'd like you to meet Dr. Joshua McClain. Dr. McClain is a friend of mine from South Carolina. He was involved in the train accident last night."

"Sorry to hear that." The two men shook hands. "Seems that wreck is causing quite a few problems today."

"What happened, Rand?"

"Your father came over to the jail to look in on Mr. Morgan, one of the engineers on the train last night. I took him into custody, for his own safety, really. He was so distraught. Threatened to kill himself." The sheriff shook his head. "Still don't know how he got hold of that knife."

Katie clutched the lawman's arm. "Is it bad?"

"He's still alive, if that's what you mean."

"I hope you'll forgive us, Sheriff, but Katie and I need to assess Dr. Clark's injuries," Josh said, pressing her toward the closed door at the end of the hall.

"I certainly understand. Guess I should be heading back to the office anyway."

Katie glanced over her shoulder at the forlorn expression on the sheriff's long face and frowned. "That was terribly rude."

Dropping his hand from her waist, Josh stopped just short of her father's bedroom door. "We can't do anything for your father listening to the sheriff give an account of what happened."

"I suppose not." Katie dropped her skirts, running her hands over the wrinkled material. "But that doesn't mean you had to be rude to him."

Josh didn't answer, just opened the door, then stood

back. Katie stepped inside, then stopped, her gaze riveted to the quiet form of her father lying on the bed while Mr. Rothchild and Mr. Anderson worked on his left thigh. His hair, usually so neatly brushed, stuck out in sharp angles around his pale face; his able hands seemed suddenly fragile against the white sheet. A deep ache settled in the pit of her stomach. When had her father gotten so old?

"Katie Bug?"

"Papa." She flew across the room, falling to her knees beside his bed, her eyes immediately drawn to the dark pooling of blood puddled beneath the man's leg. What if Papa died? How would she live without him? She took his cool hand in hers, pressing his fingers against her cheek. "Oh, Papa."

"I sent Mr. Rothchild and Mr. Anderson to get Ada." His brow crimped into a sharp wrinkle. "Something's not right."

"He's going into shock." A warm body brushed her arm, and she glanced up to find Josh draping a quilt over her father's upper body.

"He's lost a lot of blood."

Josh eyed her, his fingers already working at the knot from the makeshift tourniquet just above the gash in her father's thigh. "Whatever did this probably nicked a small artery."

Her heart contracted painfully. "Are you sure?"

"Not until I can get a better look at it." Josh released the tangle of cloth above the wound. A thick bubble of blood rose, then popped, spreading out over the thin cotton sheet. "I don't know how I can unless I retie the tourniquet, and we can't leave that on for very long without doing more damage."

"We should pack the area around the wound site with

snow," Katie said, thinking out loud. "That will stanch the blood flow long enough to give us a chance to look around."

Lifting his head, Josh flashed her a smile that made her suddenly go warm all over. "Absolutely brilliant."

"Thank you." Katie stood, feeling a bit awkward and, if she were honest with herself, a little proud. To have another doctor, or was it this doctor, acknowledge her methods sent a tiny thrill through her. She started for the door. "Let me tell Ada to get us as much clean snow as she can. And pillowcases—we can drape those over his leg so the snow doesn't damage the skin."

"No," Josh called out to her after she'd instructed Ada. "I mean, can't you go and bring back the pillowcases yourself?"

She stopped and turned to him. "Why should I do that?"

"He's your father, Kathleen. Which is why it would be best if you excused yourself from this case and let someone who's not so personally involved treat him."

"But your hands..." Her words held a hint of a challenge.

If Josh felt she'd thrown down some gauntlet, he chose to ignore it. He pulled hard against the ends of the makeshift tourniquet, his mouth flattening into a tight, painful line. "Once you cut these bandages off me, I'm sure I'll manage, but if I do run into any problems, your assistant, Ada, can help."

Blast the man! "You don't even know where to find everything." Her words stumbled as she glanced down at her father's pale white face. "And if you have to fumble around looking for needles or thread, Papa might..."

"I can show him, Katie." Katie glanced around to find

Ada Watkins standing behind her, carrying a cast-iron pot overfilled with packed snow. Although she was Katie's brightest student, Ada was still untested in urgent medical situations. What if Joshua McClain couldn't complete the surgery? What would they do then?

Josh's bandaged hands closed over her shoulders. "I know you don't like this, but you're dead on your feet. Get something to eat, even if it's just a cup of tea and a biscuit, then go rest. You've worked enough for now."

If the man weren't right, she might have considered strangling him. She looked up at him and found herself sinking into eyes as blue as the heavens. "You'll send someone to keep me updated about how he's doing?"

"As often as I can." His low baritone steadied her, giving just enough comfort without alarming her.

He's probably charmed many a lady with that voice, including me. "And when you're finished?"

"I'll come and give you a report on the operation myself."

It was a respectful answer, from one colleague to another. But her feet felt firmly nailed to the floor, emotions battling inside her. Mrs. Holden hurried in carrying buckets of snow, while Ada stuffed towels around crimson-stained sheets.

Papa's blood.

"Katie." Josh's strong voice broke through the tangle of her emotions. "Go. Now."

"Yes," she mumbled, but the fact didn't absolve the guilt she felt. If she'd only been the kind of daughter her mother had wanted her to be, the kind who would have taken care of her father's home rather than partnered with him in his practice, then…what?

Stand by and witness the suffering of others? Watch

her own father die? No, God had given her this gift for such moments as this. Whatever the circumstances, she had to trust the Lord.

Father God, I'm trusting Papa to You now, but please, Lord, please don't take him from me. Not yet.

Chapter 5

A few hours later, Josh stood over his patient, his fingers resting on the rapid pulse beating in the older man's wrist, his gaze sliding over Dr. Clark's snowy-white cheeks and pale pink lips. The surgery had gone fairly well despite the discovery of several nicks along one of the smaller arteries in Clark's thigh. Now all anyone could do was wait and pray.

Josh released the man's wrist, stretching his hands, the carbolic acid he'd used leaving dark yellowish-brown stains around the blisters. Some soap and water, along with a coating of Katie's salve, would fix him up in no time.

Josh tried to focus on the slow rise and fall of Dr. Clark's breaths, then, after realizing he'd lost count for the third time, finally gave up, his thoughts drifting back to Katie. She wasn't like any other woman he'd met at the cotillions or balls held in Charleston. No, she'd probably be bored by society or the constraints it placed on her, as much as he was. Probably too smart for most of the ladies he knew anyway, but then, she'd always been bright. That was one of the reasons they'd gotten along so well as children.

But they weren't children anymore. When had his friend grown so lovely, with her luminous dark hair that smoldered with golden fire in the sunlight and striking chocolate-brown eyes that seemed to take in everything around her? His fingers tingled at the thought of tracing the creamy outline of her jaw, and her mouth…

Bring into captivity every thought to the obedience of Christ.

Josh drew in a deep breath and exhaled. God had laid out a plan for his life, a calling that would take him to Kansas and to a group of farmers and their families who needed him. Katie was his past, an obligation their fathers had thrust on them both. She'd obviously made a life for herself here in Hillsdale, was building her own practice here. He'd do the same for himself out West.

The door opened slightly, and Ada stuck her head inside. "How's he doing?"

"Fine. He's lost a lot of blood, and we'll have to watch him for infection, but hopefully he's on the road to recovery."

"I'm sure Katie will be happy to hear that."

Why did his heart suddenly jump at her name? "Where is she?"

"In the parlor," Ada replied, leaning her head against the door frame. "She checked in on Dr. Clark's surgical patients before Mrs. Holden finally coaxed her down to the kitchen to eat. She was sitting in front of the fireplace, having a cup of tea the last time I checked."

"I need to go down and give her a report on the surgery." Josh walked the short distance to the water basin and washed his hands before tugging down his shirtsleeves, glancing around for his vest.

"Here you go, Doctor." Ada held it out.

Josh threaded his arms through the openings, then shrugged it into place. "Thank you, Ada."

She didn't respond, merely smiled at him. "How are your hands doing?"

"Not bad, though if you could round me up some of Katie's salve, I'd appreciate it," he answered, working on the buttons.

Ada opened a dresser drawer and pulled out a new set of fresh bedding. "She thought you might need some after washing up with that carbolic acid, so she made a fresh batch. Said she wanted to look at those hands again to make sure they're healing properly."

Josh smiled as he threaded the last button into the hole. *Always nursing something, aren't you, Katie Bug?* When he looked up, he caught Ada watching him, linen pressed to her chest, a knowing glint in her eye causing an uncomfortable knot to form in his stomach. "Is there something else, Ada?"

"I guess, well, congratulations."

"Excuse me?"

Color flushed the young woman's face. "Congratulations. On your engagement to Katie."

Josh felt his throat tighten. "Where did you hear that from?"

"Last night at the church, though I'm sure Mr. Woods has told it all over town by now," she continued, gently pulling the soiled towels from under Dr. Clark's wounded leg and piling them beside the bed. "Dr. C must be thrilled about the whole thing. He's been wanting Katie to settle down for a while now. Says he wants grandchildren before he gets too old to enjoy them."

"Mr. Woods." Oh, this was a bigger mess than he'd thought it would be. How had the man gotten word about their engagement around town so quickly? How could they resolve this mess without ruining Katie's good name? One step at a time, he thought, turning to the nursing assistant. "If you'll excuse me, Katie is waiting."

Stepping out into the hall, Josh closed the door, but not before one last glimpse of Ada's wide toothy smile. He hoped Katie was rested up because it was time he shared the conditions of the marriage agreement.

All of them.

The house felt eerily still to Josh as he walked downstairs, the gentle moans of the steps under his weight the only sounds. A lone lantern in the hallway did little to chase the gray shadows that filled the cracks and crevices of the room, giving it a doomed feel that matched his mood.

How had he landed in this mess, with the whole town knowing of their engagement? Josh scrubbed rough fingers through his hair. His father's attorney had told him to leave well enough alone, go to Kansas, make a life. What could Clark do, Mr. Bingham had said, sue his father for breach of promise, try to collect monies lost years ago?

But Bingham's words were as tainted as his father's. Josh hung on the last stair step. He may not agree with the marriage contract, but he would handle the repercussions better than running away. He owed it to himself and

Katie to be honest. He wouldn't be forced into marrying someone not of his own choosing, and neither should she.

Then why did the thought of Katie married to someone else bother him?

Probably some leftover possessiveness he felt from their friendship. After all, they had been very close. All Josh knew was that Katie deserved someone special, someone who appreciated her intelligence and uniqueness, who would love her for who she was, not what society thought she should be. Someone who would honor her until the day she died. Nothing less would do.

Not for Katie.

Unsure where the parlor was, he noticed a flicker of light dancing along the top of the arched entranceway to his right. Had Katie lit a candle or did the fire in the fireplace need attention? He stepped into the room and saw splashes of Katie everywhere: in the tiny figurines of dogs and other animals gracing the tabletop; in the tomes of books gathered neatly in the bookshelves; in the high-backed chair tucked into the corner, a perfect place for her to curl up and practice her sutures or read the latest medical studies.

But where was the woman in question?

A small sigh from the fireplace drew Josh's attention to the sofa. He walked around, then sat down on the hearth, his eyes resting on the woman sleeping in front of him. He'd seen her like this before, as a girl curled up with whatever ailing beast she was nursing at that moment.

But nothing compared to this image of Katie, her hands folded neatly under one rosy cheek, her hair a tangled mess of curls falling over the delicate curve of her shoulder. She must have changed her dress, for the skirts gathered into a neat tuck at her trim waist. Beyond the yards of cloth and petticoats, two trim stocking feet peeked out, her boots warming on the hearth beside him.

Her lips parted on another sigh, and Josh wanted to lean down and brush his mouth against hers. Instead, he gently pushed her hair back off of her face. “Katie.”

Her eyes fluttered, as if warring between sleep and consciousness, before finally opening. “Josh?”

He sat back then, not wanting to embarrass her or himself with his reaction to this new Katie, this very womanly Katie. “Did you sleep well?”

She sat up quickly, touching her feet to the floor, and then, having realized she was in her stocking feet, tucked them under her skirts. “I just closed my eyes for a bit.”

“You were tired.”

“How’s Papa? How did the surgery go?”

“Good,” Josh replied. “We’ll have to watch him for infection and keep him still for the next couple of weeks, but he’s strong. He should do just fine.”

Katie slumped back into the cushions, her eyes closing in relief. “Thank You, Lord!”

Yes, thank You, Lord! Josh added silently.

The tinkling of cups and silverware drew Josh and Katie’s attention to the doorway as Mrs. Holden bustled into the room. She laid the coffee service along with a plate of freshly baked biscuits on the table beside Katie. “These biscuits are just out of the oven, so be careful. Don’t need anyone else around here getting hurt.”

“Thank you, Mrs. Holden.” Katie waited until the older woman was out of earshot before turning to Josh. “You’ll have to excuse Mrs. Holden. This whole thing with Papa has upset her greatly.”

Josh tossed a hot biscuit onto his plate, then added

a heap of butter and strawberry jelly on the side. "Are they...?" Then he added, "I'm sorry. That's none of my business."

"That's all right. They haven't declared themselves yet, but I think there are tender feelings on each side."

"Your father doesn't come across as the type of man to wait for anyone." Josh broke off a piece of the biscuit and tossed it in his mouth, moaning as it melted into a delicious buttery bite. "Especially if the woman can cook like this. This is wonderful!"

"Maybe you ought to tell me more about the surgery." Katie gave him an uncomfortable smile.

Had he said something wrong? She'd only seemed to grow uneasy when the topic of Mrs. Holden and her father had come up. Was that it? Did Katie object to her father's feelings for the cook? And, if so, why?

"Would you like another cup of coffee?"

Josh shook his head. "I'm going to get some more wood."

"Well, I could certainly use a cup." Katie stood and walked over to the service, willing this uncomfortable knot in the pit of her stomach to resolve. A coolness that had nothing to do with the fire had settled between them in the past half hour. Was it that Josh wanted to remain detached while they discussed her father's surgery? No, it had started with the conversation about her father and Mrs. Holden, but why? Had he wanted to know more about her father and Mrs. Holden? Though, from what she remembered, Josh was never one for gossip. But what more could she tell him? That she feared she was the only reason her father hadn't married Mrs. Holden yet, worried that Katie couldn't survive on her own?

I'm pathetic, she thought, and poured herself a cup, dropping in two sugar lumps before adding a generous splash of cream. Lifting her cup and saucer, she turned and met Josh's dark blue gaze, almost faltering at the hint of quiet humor dancing in his eyes. She refused to let him get the best of her. "What is it?"

He nodded toward her cup. "You still like a little bit of coffee with your milk, don't you?"

Her breath froze in her lungs. Why had Josh remembered such an intimate detail about her? And why did the thought have such an effect on her pulmonary system, particularly her lungs?

One side of his mouth rose into a crooked smile that seemed to melt something frozen inside her. "Your mother always feared you'd drink your father's herd dry."

Katie drew in a slow breath. Of course her mother had said such a thing, along with bemoaning the numerous sick animals Katie had brought home, or scolding her over the tears in her petticoats from climbing up a tree with Josh. She'd never be the kind of lady her mother had wanted her to be, a genteel woman with the beauty and manners to take Charleston society by storm. Was that why her father had signed that silly marriage agreement with Samuel McClain? Had he been so sure even then that Katie would never attract a husband on her own?

She stared hard at Josh. But why had Mr. McClain agreed to it? Had Josh come to Hillsdale to honor the agreement? There was only one way to find out. "Why are you here, Josh?"

He blinked, then chuckled softly. "You've always been straight to the point, haven't you?"

"I find it's always the best way to be." Though at the moment, her heart wouldn't agree. Just these few short hours with Josh had reminded her of the friendship she'd lost; the companionship, the tiny intimacies that had branded them as friends. That Josh was someone who accepted her as herself.

"Come. Sit down beside me."

Katie shook her head. He'd be close enough for her to feel the warmth radiating from his body, smell his scent of soap, wool and masculinity. It was just too dangerous to her heart. "Just tell me."

Josh stood. Pacing around the room, he started to scrub his injured hand over his neck, then thought better of it, dropping it to his side. "I thought I should come and talk to you in person about the contract our fathers drew up."

It was the honorable thing to do, though it couldn't be comfortable for him, traveling all this way just to do right by her. "Our fathers want us to marry."

"It would seem."

He wouldn't reject her outright. Josh was too kind to do such a thing. So she must be the one to put an end to this nonsense. "And if I don't agree to abide by the contract?"

Josh seemed to force himself to look at her, his gaze catching and holding hers. "There's a situation in regard to your dowry."

He'd mentioned the dowry before, as if it was important. "What about it?"

"As part of the agreement," Josh said, hesitating, "your father was required to give my father a bank draft at the time the contract was signed."

The cup and saucer slid with a jangle back down on the service. Bad enough her father felt the need to contract a marriage with Josh's father, but to pay him to sign it. That was what Josh meant by being bought and paid for! How could Papa have embarrassed her like this, and with her dearest friend?

Warm fingers slid over her elbow, taking gentle siege of her arm. Josh's tender voice compelled her. "Come. Sit down."

Katie followed, her emotions tangled in an uncompromising knot, growing tighter until she thought her heart would burst. And poor Josh! Thrown into the midst of the disappointment she'd caused her parents. "I'm so sorry."

"What for?" He pulled her down on the couch, wrapping his arm around her as he used to when one of her animal "patients" had died. "It seems as if our fathers are to blame for this."

"But to pay someone to marry me." She buried her heated face in his shoulder, instantly aware of the solid mass of muscle flexing beneath her cheek. Katie tried to lean back, but Josh's arm tightened around her until finally, she rested her head against him, relaxing into his strength.

Long moments stretched out. The wood in the fireplace popped. They weren't going to come up with any type of solution to this problem simply sitting here. Katie pushed away from him, Josh giving little resistance as she moved to the other side of the couch. "What do you think we ought to do?"

"There is an easy solution."

"What's that?"

Josh glanced at her, and for one brief moment, she was lost in what might have been if she and her father had stayed in South Carolina, if her friendship with Josh had been allowed to blossom naturally into something more. But then he spoke, and all those hopes were dashed. "Do you want to marry me?"

Chapter 6

The question came out before Josh could call it back. Didn't he want out of this marriage agreement? Wasn't that why he'd come all this way, to get Katie and her father to agree to his terms? Then why had he asked her to marry him?

And why was it taking so long for her to respond?

"Did that blow to your head cause more damage than just a black eye?" She studied him, her brown eyes focused on him. "Because you talk as if you've lost your mind."

Was that it? Was he concussed? No, but the other alternative seemed just as far-fetched. "I'm fine."

Katie sat back, her arms wrapped around her waist as if to protect herself, but from what? Him? "Then why did you ask me that...question?"

Josh was still trying to figure that out himself. "You didn't answer me."

She pressed her lips together. "No, I will not marry you."

Josh let go of the breath he'd been holding, relief flowing through him. But along with it came something else, some unnamed emotion that put a damper on the moment. Maybe it was just his male pride at having his very first marriage proposal turned down so decisively. "Then we need to think of a way out of this mess."

"Right." She leaned into the couch cushions. "You said your father accepted a bank draft when the contract was signed. What if he gives it back?"

Josh stared into the fireplace. He'd come up with that idea, too, until Father had revealed the extent of his folly. "It can't be returned, at least not at the moment."

"I don't understand."

"Father wasted that money and everything else after Mother died." He choked out the words as if they left a bitter taste in his mouth. "All that's left is the McClain name, and that won't be worth much once people realize the truth."

Katie curled her hand over his. "Well, what's done is done. There's no reason to ruin our lives over a few coins."

Ruin their lives! Didn't she understand that until this debt was repaid, he couldn't begin building his life? "There's many a good reason for your father to expect repayment, the first being my family's honor. I won't be able to live with myself if I don't make this right."

Her temper flared. "And I won't be made anyone's obligation."

Josh stared at her. His wasn't the only pride at stake here. Lifting his hand to her face, he caught a stray curl that had escaped her chignon, twisting it around his finger. "That came out wrong, didn't it?"

"Yes, it did."

Josh let go of the curl, watching it spring back into place, brushing against her cheek. Without thinking, he followed its path, tracing his finger down the line of her jaw before letting his hand drop away. Why did he feel so drawn to her? And what was that pathetic excuse for a marriage proposal really about? "I'm sorry."

"Me, too," she replied, pushing her hair behind her ear, her fingers lingering on the soft pink shell. "I don't know about you, but I'm too tired to come up with anything right now. Why don't we put this aside for the moment and go check on your trunks?"

Josh nodded. It wouldn't do to make such an important decision in haste. "I've been wondering how my equipment fared through the wreck."

Katie opened her mouth to speak, but a pounding at the front door drew their attention. Josh followed her into the hallway, the quiet sway of her skirts as she hurried to the door bringing a faint grimace to his mouth. This grown-up Katie was just as appealing as her younger version, maybe even more.

Make my thoughts Your thoughts, Lord.

"Where is my wife?" A rough-looking man plowed past Katie, his gaze flittering from one place to another before finally coming to rest on him. Grabbing his hat by the front brim, he scraped it off his head in one fluid movement before planting himself in front of Josh. "Are you Dr. Clark?"

He glanced over the man's shoulder to see Mr. Woods had joined Katie at the door. "Sorry to barge in like this, but Mr. McDaniels has been looking all over town for his wife. I figured we better try here."

"Of course," Katie replied. "She's upstairs."

"Is she all right?" The man stared at Josh as if only he could give him answers. "They said if she was brought here, she probably needed surgery."

The soft swish of petticoats announced Katie's nearness. When she spoke, it was with a tenderness of one who cared deeply. "Mrs. McDaniels was resting comfortably last time I checked."

"Begging your pardon, ma'am, but I'd rather hear what Dr. Clark has to say."

The hairs on the back of Josh's neck rose, an overwhelming need to protect Katie curling inside him. "I'm Dr. McClain."

Confusion flashed in McDaniels's eyes. "But everyone told me I needed to speak to Dr. Clark. Where is he?"

"There are two Dr. Clarks, Mr. McDaniels," Katie started, her head tilted to the side almost apologetically. "I've taken over your wife's case since my father was injured this morning. If you would like to come into the parlor, we can discuss your wife's condition."

"There's only one name on the sign, a Dr. Ethan Clark," the man snapped.

"That's my father."

"But Katie here's graduated, and at the top of her class, too," Woods injected as he closed the door and hurried toward them. "Been working with her papa ever since."

"I don't want some woman who doesn't know what she's doing doctoring my wife." McDaniels crumpled up the brim of his hat. "I want a real doctor."

Josh felt his muscles tighten. Katie didn't deserve to be treated with such disrespect, not after the night and morning she'd put in. He started to tell the man so when Katie spoke. "Mr. McDaniels, I'm sure you've been very worried and would probably feel better if you saw your wife. I can show you to her room if you like."

The man stepped back. "Just tell me which one it is."

"First door to your left. One of my father's students, Mr. Deavers, is sitting with her right now."

The man hardly waited for Katie's instructions before bounding up the stairs, taking two at a time.

"Told your papa he needed to get that sign taken care of," Woods said, breaking the silence. "Just not right that your name isn't up there alongside his."

Katie gave him a faint smile. "You know the reason why Papa didn't want to do that. And it wouldn't have made a difference with Mr. McDaniels anyway."

Something in the casual way she answered bothered Josh. "Are you treated like this often?"

She didn't answer, just lowered her gaze to the threadbare rug at her feet.

"Well, if you won't answer, I will," Woods said, giving his head a sharp nod. "Yes."

"Woody!"

"Well, it's so, ain't it?" Woods asked, tugging at his gray beard in irritation. "That's the reason why her papa won't have her name put on the sign out front. Says it doesn't matter. Thinks the town council will eventually come around and start paying Katie for her service, but it hasn't happened so far."

Josh wasn't much for violence, but right now, he wanted to punch something. How could Ethan Clark do this to his daughter, after all she'd gone through to graduate from medical school? Did he realize what a fine physician she was, what a fine woman she was, to so callously toss her feelings to the wind? And why was she taking her father's side in this? Where was that girl who fought to save every injured or abused creature? Didn't she know she was worth so much more?

"Please. Stop, Woody." Katie held up her hand. "As much as I'd like to change everyone's mind, I can't. I have to show them I'm worth a paycheck. Now, why don't you go in the kitchen and get something to eat? I'm sure Mrs. Holden has some biscuits left over."

Woods nodded, drawing Katie loosely in his arms. "You know your papa thinks you're the best doctor there is, now, don't you?"

The brief nod seemed to satisfy the older man because he gave her a slight squeeze, then let her go and headed for the kitchen. But Josh knew Katie too well to be convinced. "McDaniels shouldn't have treated you that way."

"Maybe not," she conceded. "But I figure his day hasn't been much better than mine. And the next few days may end up being the worst in his life." Katie's eyes brimmed with worry when she lifted her face to his. "His wife is dying."

Carrying her boots in one hand and her skirts in the other, Katie crept quietly down the front steps the next morning, the cold morning air causing her toes to curl inside her wool stockings. No sense waking up the entire house when the sun hadn't even poked its head up yet.

Last night had been a definite improvement on the previous evening. After Mr. McDaniels had left, she and Josh had gone to the train station only to discover his trunks wouldn't be recovered until the next afternoon. They had hurried to the mercantile, where old Mr. Varner had extended his store hours to accommodate those in the accident. No one had spoken about the rumor going around, but Mrs. Varner had winked at her while Josh had gathered a few necessities.

By the time they'd arrived back home, Papa had been awake, weak and still groggy from the laudanum and blood loss. Kate had checked the bandage, aware of Mrs. Holden bustling around the room, filling the water pitcher and plumping the pillows, the woman's gaze straying every now and again to the bed where Papa lay.

And then there was Josh. Poor man, coming all the way here to Hillsdale to deal with this marriage contract in an honorable way, and getting caught up in all this. After the patients had settled in for the night, Katie had sat him down at the kitchen table and bathed his hands before coating his palms with her homemade salve. They had talked well into the night, about their childhood, about the years apart. It had felt good being with Josh, not the awkward, tongue-tied memories of her last year in Abbeville.

But now, a new morning dawned, and Katie had to get back to her life here in Hillsdale. She needed time alone to think, to sort through these new feelings Josh's arrival had unleashed in her, and maybe, just maybe, come up with a solution to this marriage mess. Katie hurried over to the coatrack, glancing through the pile of coats, scarves and hats. Where was her cape?

"Sneaking out without me?"

Katie clutched her boots to her chest as she turned. Josh leaned against the parlor doorway, his arms folded neatly around his waist. He wore the same dark blue suit as he had since the wreck, but his shirt was new, his collar and shirtsleeves with crisp corners. His blond hair had been tamed away from his face, though just barely, and the pale gold bristles that had lined his jaw last night had been shaved clean.

My, but the man was handsome! Katie forced herself to breathe. "What are you doing up so early?"

"Couldn't sleep. Had a lot on my mind."

So, she hadn't been the only one tossing and turning last night. "Anything I can do to help?"

"Keep me busy." He shrugged, dropping his arms and taking a step toward her. "I figured with your father unavailable, you might need help doing rounds."

Spending more time with Josh might not be a good idea. Not that she didn't trust him; she did, more than anyone else on this earth, save her papa. But spending time with him, working closely with him, might be more than her poor heart could take. "You may not get breakfast until almost noon."

"I can make do with a cup of coffee."

Oh, dear. Another thing they had in common. "You sure? It's cold out there, may even be snowing again."

Heat rose in her cheeks as he studied her. "You make rounds by yourself, don't you?"

How did he…? Katie's back stiffened. "Papa teaches morning classes over at the college, so I do the early rounds, yes."

"Is that the only way…?" He hesitated as if he'd thought better of it.

Katie felt her muscles loosen slightly. Did it really matter what Josh thought of her father's plan to get the town to accept her as their doctor? Yes, she might be an old maid before it happened, but there wasn't anything else—or anyone—for her to consider. A faint hint of disappointment slid through her.

Something else for her to think about.

"Planning on carrying your boots with you?"

"Oh!" She hurried over to the bench, heat spreading up her neck and bursting into her cheeks. Jamming her feet into the soft leather, she reached for the strings, her fingers fumbling with the ties as if she were a little girl trying to tie her first knot.

"Here." Kneeling down in front of her, Josh brushed her hands away, a smile playing along his lips. The heat from his fingers radiated through the leather to her ankle as he cupped it in one palm and rested her booted foot on his thigh. "You never were one for staying in your shoes."

"You always had me down at the Johnsons' creek, fishing or hunting for frogs or something." Katie stiffened, each pull of the boot strings a gentle tug on her heart. "Mama never could understand why I had wet skirts but dry stockings and shoes."

"Did I get you in trouble a lot?"

"Maybe," she replied, putting her hand over her mouth when a chuckle threatened to burst out. "But I wouldn't have missed those moments for all the snow in Michigan."

Josh gave her a troubled smile. "Still, your mama couldn't have been real happy with me."

"Mama loved you." Katie picked up the bonnet that lay at the end of the bench and gave the rich velvet a couple of swipes. "Thing is, she never was truly happy with me."

She stilled. Why in the world had she said that? It might be true, but the last thing she wanted to talk about was her mother's disappointment in her.

"You'll need this." Josh held out her cape.

"Thank you." She clutched the heavy wool in her grasp and stood, swinging the cape in a small circle until it came to rest on her shoulders. She should have known

Josh would understand these feelings she had about her mother; he always had even when they were children. Katie had come to an understanding years ago that, while she couldn't change the memory of her mother's indifference, she had to change her reaction to it. It was the only way she could live the life God desired for her.

Katie glanced up at Josh. Did that life include this man?

Pulling her calfskin gloves out of her pockets, Katie tugged them on. "Your eye is looking better. The swelling has gone down quite a bit and the bruises are turning a dark blue."

"Good." He met her gaze, his blue eyes shining with a teasing sparkle. "Maybe I won't scare the patients, then."

Handsome and funny. It was a wonder how the man had remained unmarried. Had the marriage contract their fathers had arranged kept Josh from his true love? Was the lady he'd chosen waiting for news that the contract was null and void, and now their life together could begin?

Do not worry about tomorrow, for tomorrow will have its own worries. Sufficient for each day is its own troubles.

Thank You, Lord! Your Words just when I need them! Tying the ribbons of her bonnet into a stylish bow, Katie collected her medical bag and followed Josh to the door.

The next hour passed in a slow blur. Most of her patients complained of being sore and stiff, but that was to be expected after being tossed around during the wreck. A couple of days' rest, and Katie expected most of the passengers to be ready to travel.

The snow started to fall again as they walked down the front path leading from the Steeds' home, having just bid Mrs. Steed goodbye. Josh remained close to her side, drawing her hand through the crook of one arm while he held her medical bag in the other.

"I can see why you became a doctor," Josh finally said.

Katie chuckled. "That's a switch. Most people are too busy telling me why I shouldn't be one."

"I'm serious. And if any of those people would just open their eyes, they'd see what a wonderful physician you are in your own right."

She tilted her head to glance at him, expecting to see a flicker of humor in his eyes or a smile teasing his lips. But his expression was serious, even respectful, while his gaze shone with an intense pride. "You really think so?"

"Why are you so surprised?" Josh gave her a wide smile. "You've been doctoring for as long as I've known you."

"But that was just dogs and cats and birds and..."

"The least of God's creatures, and you didn't think twice about caring for them. The Lord was preparing you to go into medicine even then, Kathleen Clark."

Emotions knotted in her throat. Katie had never thought of it like that, considered that God would be so patient with her, would allow her to have the dream of her heart. She felt precious, cherished, as if she were a child cuddled up in her father's lap, his strong arms cradling her, protecting her from harm. But wasn't that what she was, His beloved child?

"Thank you." Without thinking, Katie stood up on her toes, her hands resting on Josh's shoulders as she pressed her cheek against his. The arm she'd been holding snaked around her waist, holding her tightly to him. Probably so their feet wouldn't slip out from under them, she thought, resting her head against his chest.

"You're welcome," he replied on a husky breath. Something soft whispered against her hair, almost like a kiss, but before she could respond, Josh gently pushed her out of his arms.

As well he should. Katie backed up a step, the ground underneath her slippery. "I'm so sorry. I shouldn't have flown at you like that."

"You don't have to apologize." The dark gleam in his eyes set her pulse racing. "In fact, if you ever want to throw yourself at me like that again, I'll be happy to oblige."

The man was an incorrigible flirt! And handsome, considerate, smart and funny. But he wasn't the type to be forced into marriage, no matter what their fathers' wishes might be. Why should he, when what he probably wanted was the same thing she did, someone he could love, who would share his life, give him children?

That Katie had found those things in him was her own foolish problem.

"Katie, Dr. McClain?" Rand Dawes hurried toward them, snow dusting his shoulders and the rim of his hat. "I've been looking all over for you."

Worry niggled through her. "What's wrong? It isn't Papa, is it?"

He shook his head. "Mrs. Holden was getting ready to feed him his breakfast when I got there. No, I was looking for Dr. McClain here."

"What for?" Josh asked.

The sheriff shifted from one boot to the other, his mouth pulled into a tight line, as if he'd eaten something that had left a sour taste in his mouth. Then he straightened. "I just came from the train station. I hate to tell you this, Doc, but all your belongings that were in the baggage car were destroyed in the fire."

Chapter 7

Gone.

Josh stepped out onto the train platform and closed the door behind him. Everything, gone. His medical books, his equipment, even the linens for his patient beds, destroyed by the fire in the mail car. *I don't understand, Lord. I was following Your will. Why would You allow this to happen?*

Warmth slid across his palm, tightening around his hand in a caress. He glanced down to find Katie's gloved fingers twining with his. "I'm so sorry, Josh."

He nodded, not ready for condolences, not when his dreams had just been lost and there was still so much to do. "I wonder how long it's going to take to get an answer from Mr. Mabry. He's going to need to talk to the other farmers before he makes any decisions."

"Did you tell him that the railroad intends to reimburse you for your losses?"

Still holding her hand, Josh started walking down the platform, Katie close to his side. "It wouldn't matter. These men are on a very specific time line. Even if the railroad gave me a bank draft today, I'd still have to order new equipment, and that could take months."

"Not necessarily, not if you just get the essentials."

Josh glanced down at Katie, noting the tiny line of concentration that had formed between her dark brows. She was something special, this dearest friend. Though friendship didn't explain the possessiveness he'd felt holding her in his arms, brushing his lips against her soft curls. Better to tease her than ponder those thoughts. "Are you trying to figure out a way to be rid of me?"

But Katie refused to rise to the bait. "No, I'm… Well, to be honest with you, I'm running an inventory of our equipment in my head, trying to figure out what we could spare."

The woman really was trying to get rid of him! Josh turned, suddenly irritated. "I'm not taking your equipment."

Her eyes widened. "Why not?"

"Because…" He mashed his lips together. Charity usually had costly strings attached, at least among his father's acquaintances. So, what would Katie want? "I can wait for Southern Michigan to make amends. If Mabry and his group want to hire another doctor before that happens, then I'm sure another position will come open."

"But why should you lose this opportunity when I want to help?"

Josh let go of her hand, a slight chill running up the length of his arm at the loss of her warmth. If she didn't understand that agreeing to her help would only make breaking the marriage contract more difficult, then he wasn't about to explain it. A man had his pride, and this whole situation had already taken several shots at his.

Josh took the steps down to the sidewalk, fully expecting to turn around and find Katie gone. But she caught up with him, though she walked an arm's length away and muttered something about "a stubborn old mule."

Maybe he'd read the situation wrong. Maybe all Katie did want to do was help. She knew the McClains had no money; he'd told her as much, but that hadn't seemed to bother her like it would the other young ladies in their old Charleston set.

Well, he couldn't be beholden to her anyway, not with the debt of Katie's dowry hanging over his head. If the job in Kansas fell through, he'd head to Chicago and see if he could secure a job at one of the hospitals. Then every few weeks, he could hop a train to Hillsdale and visit Katie. And pay Dr. Clark back the money his father had lost.

So why didn't one or two visits a month seem enough?

Josh grimaced. What was happening here? Katie had been his best friend, was his best friend even now. But when she'd been in his arms, her head pillowed on his shoulder, it had felt like more. Never had he felt so protective, possessive. He wanted to be the man Katie thought he was, see the world through her eyes. Yes, they were friends, but did it feel like something else, something like love?

He needed to think. "I could use a cup of coffee about now."

"Ursula's is just down the street here. She's probably got a pot on." If she was still angry with him, she hid it well.

"Ursula?"

"Ursula and Josef Bentz. They're friends of mine that

run a boardinghouse for students enrolled at Hillsdale." A ghost of a smile hovered around her lips. "I tutor Papa's students there most afternoons."

The thought didn't sit well with Josh, remembering the number of male students following behind Katie the night of the wreck. Like a pack of wolves hunting down their next prey. "And the ladies?"

She chuckled. "I believe Lady Principal Whipple would be aghast at the idea of her pupils studying adult human anatomy alongside the men."

"But she has no qualms about you teaching with your father? That's odd."

Katie grimaced, her shoulders stiff. "As I'm not a paid employee of the college and simply volunteer my time to help some of Papa's struggling students, Miss Whipple has no jurisdiction over my activities."

Josh felt his temper flare again. Didn't these people realize what they had in Katie? A doctor with no practice. A teacher with no school. What kind of message did that send to the young women enrolled at Hillsdale?

The dwelling seemed unusually quiet for a boardinghouse when Katie showed Josh into the front hall, stamping her boots against the worn throw rug covering the hardwood floor. She pulled on her ribbons, glancing in one room, then another. "I wonder where everyone is. Ursula? Josef?"

He shucked off his coat, then hung it and his hat on one of the wooden knobs on the wall. "I thought you said all the boarders are students."

"They are," Katie answered, tugging the scarf from her neck. "They must have had class this afternoon. But Ursula usually meets me at the front door. Maybe she's out back in the kitchen." She walked a few steps down the narrow hallway toward the back part of the house, then turned back to him. "There's a fireplace in the dining hall if you want to get warm while I check."

The need to thaw out pulled him into the dining area, though he did linger a few extra moments to watch Katie's trim figure glide down the hall. The room was larger than he'd thought from the outside, long and narrow, as if the back walls of the house had been taken off at some point and rooms added. Four wide oak tables took up most of the space, perfect for meals and study time. The buttercream walls and lacy yellow curtains and the oversize brick fireplace that took up most of the opposite wall gave the place a homey feeling.

This would be a perfect waiting room, Josh thought, walking to the table nearest the fireplace and pulling out a chair. He would have an open table for parents to gather with their children, and line the other walls with comfortable chairs for family members to wait during surgery. It was kind of large for one doctor, but perfect for a married couple setting up practice.

Lord, I'm going to Kansas, remember?

"She and Josef are probably delivering food to some of the families around town." Katie swiped her hand gently across her hair as she maneuvered around the tables. Josh rose and pulled out the chair next to his, waiting until she was settled before sitting back down. "I'm sure they'll be back in a moment."

"So, we're unchaperoned?" Josh glanced around, as if suddenly realizing just how alone they were.

"You needn't worry that I'm trying to spring some trap on you, Josh." Katie laughed. "Being a female doctor has pretty much left my reputation in tatters as it is."

Didn't the woman know how much danger that kind

of attitude could get her into? Especially tutoring a room full of men, on human anatomy, no less! Josh scooted his chair closer to hers. "What if *I'm* setting a trap for *you?*"

She leaned her chin against her fisted hand, her smile taunting him. "I don't believe you."

Maybe he'd been wrong. Maybe Katie only felt friendship for him after all. He leaned in closer. "Why's that?"

Katie bit her lower lip and swallowed. Hard. "The marriage contract."

Blast their fathers for coming up with that piece of garbage! If God had chosen Katie for him, he didn't want that marriage agreement hanging over their union. "Yeah, well, what if I wanted to kiss you?"

Bright pink blossoms bloomed in her cheeks, but she surprised him when she inched toward him, her eyes searching his, a hint of a teasing smile on her lips. "You're not serious."

Someone needed to teach Katie a lesson about the dangers of being alone with a man. Who better than him? He was her friend, after all. Capturing her chin between his fingers, he tilted her head up, their gazes meeting, tangling before her eyes fell shut. "I've never been more serious in my life, Katie."

"Josh." He could hear the challenge in her words, as if she was daring him as she had all those times when they were just children.

And he was never one to turn down a dare. Closing the space between them, he settled his lips over hers.

Oh, mercy!

Katie had spent her whole twenty-four years wondering what all the fuss was about, but as Josh's hands cupped her face, angling her head slightly, it felt right that her first kiss belonged to him.

"Mrs. Bentz, is this how you conduct business in your boardinghouse?"

Josh lifted his head, the muscles under Katie's palms going rigid as he drew her against his chest. Heat flushed through her from embarrassment…or more likely from the bubbles of joy bursting through her veins.

"Principal Whipple, I know Dr. Clark has a very good explanation."

Elizabeth Whipple. Of all the people to catch them in such a compromising position. Katie had made the mistake of believing the principal of female students would be more accepting of her decision to become a physician, but she'd been very wrong. Miss Whipple thought Katie was an oddity, a distraction for young ladies who wanted an education in the gentler arts.

"Let me take care of this," Josh whispered.

Hadn't he already done enough as it was? Trying to scare her as if she were some untried schoolgirl going to her first dance! But try as she might, she couldn't be angry with him, not when her lips still tingled from his kiss. Not when she wished he would kiss her again.

"Dr. Clark, I'm waiting for an explanation."

Josh moved beside her, his fingers curved around her elbow as he lifted her out of the chair. Her legs felt as if the bones had turned into a jar of Ursula's apple jelly. She locked her knees, but they seemed equally unsteady. "I'm so sorry, Principal Whipple. I don't really have an explanation for my behavior."

"I'm sorry, Miss Whipple, is it?" Josh interrupted, giving her a brief smile, then turning toward the ladies standing in the doorway. "I beg your pardon for our, my, unseemly behavior. It's just a man should have the right to kiss his fiancée, especially when they've been separated as long as we have."

The room began to sway. Had Josh just called her his fiancée?

"Oh! So that's what Mr. Woody was speaking of!" Ursula exclaimed, a huge smile lighting her face as she turned to Miss Whipple. "He told my Josef that Katie's betrothed had been injured in the train wreck, but as she had never talked to me or Liberty about it, I thought Mr. Woody might be mistaken."

"No mistake about it," Josh added, dropping Katie's elbow to circle her waist, drawing her close to his side. "It's been settled upon for several years."

That much was true. But what was going to happen when Josh moved on, and she was forced to face the sympathetic stares and the not-so-discreet sidestepping of a broken engagement? She'd never earn the town's or the college's respect, not with a broken betrothal in her past.

Principal Whipple stared over the top of her silver-rimmed glasses. "And who might you be?"

Katie blanched. Mama would've had her hide for forgetting the introductions. "I'm so sorry, Miss Whipple, Mrs. Bentz. This is Dr. Joshua McClain, an old family friend from Charleston. Josh, this is Elizabeth Whipple, lady principal at the college, and Mrs. Ursula Bentz, proprietor of this lovely establishment."

"So very nice to meet some of Katie's friends."

"McClain? And you were in the train wreck?" Miss Whipple asked.

Why would she ask such a question? Katie nodded. "Josh was coming in from Cleveland."

A smile exploded across Miss Whipple's face. "Then

you're the gentleman my darling Ginger has been going on about."

Katie waited for him to reply. Josh didn't seem the type to preen and get all puffed up, but then, most men she knew liked to go on about such things. "How is she?"

"Her shoulder was dislocated, but Dr. McClain repositioned it." Elizabeth flashed Katie a curt smile before turning back to Josh. "She wears her sling like a badge of honor."

"She's a brave little girl."

Miss Whipple took a step toward them, clutching her reticule tightly in her hands. "She says you saved her life."

Katie stole a glance at Josh, faintly surprised by the rosy hue settling high in his cheeks. "I just kept her company. God is the only one with the power to save us, Miss Whipple."

Katie had forgotten that about him, his endearing humbleness, never taking credit, trying to always give God the glory. Oh, he failed at times; he was only human. But he succeeded in turning the focus on the Lord more times than not.

"Have you set a date for the wedding yet?"

And just when I think it's going so well, Lord.

Katie felt a slight tremor go through Josh, and she almost smirked. Now he was nervous; well, served him right after the pins and needles she'd been feeling since Ursula and Miss Whipple had interrupted that kiss. But when Katie looked up at him, the calm blue waters of his eyes lulled her into a sense of security, as if to say he'd never let her face the repercussions alone.

"I would think with Dr. Clark laid up, Katie isn't

thinking wedding dates right now," Ursula answered. "Isn't that right, Katie?"

She blinked, her muddled mind clearing just a bit. "That's right. I couldn't think of getting married without my father to give me away."

"And," Ursula added, "Liberty would need time to make Katie the wedding dress of her dreams."

Miss Whipple's skeptical expression seemed to soften. "Well, then, I guess congratulations are in order. But, Dr. Clark, please remember that we are responsible for very impressionable young ladies, and refrain from displays of affection until a more private time and place, or there will be repercussions." She shook her head in disapproval, but a brief emotion flickered in her eyes, something Katie couldn't quite put her finger on that made her wonder about the principal, almost feel sorry for her.

"Mrs. Bentz, I have some responsibilities back at the college that require me to cut this meeting short. If you'll excuse me."

Ursula shot Katie a confused look before nodding to Miss Whipple. "Certainly."

When Ursula led the lady principal out into the hall, Josh turned to face Katie. "I'm sorry about that."

"Which part?" She paced in a small circle near the fireplace, the thud of her boots seeming to vibrate against the walls. "Telling Elizabeth Whipple that you're my fiancé—" her tongue grew thick, heat rippling through her veins at the memory "—or kissing me."

"Katie."

His voice halted her in her tracks. She glanced up at him, his eyes dark and unreadable, and she lifted her chin just a bit to escape their web. "What?"

She had barely blinked when he was standing in front

of her, the scent of clean soap and fresh air filling her nose. He didn't touch her, simply stood there until she couldn't stop herself from looking at him.

Josh gave her a faint smile. "If you want me to tell you I'm sorry for kissing you, I can't."

He should apologize. That would be the gentlemanly thing to do. And if she were the calm, levelheaded woman she'd always been, Katie wouldn't feel this thrill of feminine pride at his admission. Instead, she surprised herself. "I'm not sorry either."

He moved closer. "Really?"

Katie stepped back, her hip brushing against the table behind her. Distancing herself from him now would be better for both of them; he had a practice waiting for him in Kansas and she… Well, she wasn't sure what life held for her once news of this afternoon spread around town. But God had a plan for her, for them both, and she had to trust it.

Josh must have understood because he remained quiet, unmoving. But the liveliness had left his expression, the spark that had been in his eyes dulled to what she thought was disappointment.

The soft swish of fabric announced Ursula's return. "I'm so sorry, Katie. Principal Whipple cornered me at Mr. Varner's with some problem with the students. If I'd known…"

"I'm the one who should apologize." Katie rushed across the room, taking the older woman by the hands. While a few ladies had accepted her as their doctor, most refused to socialize with her. But Ursula and Josef had welcomed her as if they'd always known her. And how had she repaid their kindness? By acting unseemly in their home. "I'm so sorry. I don't know what I was thinking. Did Miss Whipple say anything about it when you walked her to the door?"

"Only that she hoped you married soon for the sake of your papa's students."

"I don't understand." Katie leaned back, glancing at Josh before returning her attention to Ursula. "What does that mean?"

The woman's gaze shifted from Josh, then back to Katie. "Until you exchange vows with Dr. McClain, you're forbidden from tutoring any of the students here. If she finds you here, Josef and I will lose our boarders. And your papa will be sacked."

"Katie, I'm so sorry." Josh reached out to her.

She shrugged him away. What had she been thinking? She should have known better, should have remembered her future was at stake. "Don't you need to get back to the house and write up that list of items you lost in the train wreck?"

"Katie."

"I'll be home in a little while."

Josh gave her a brief nod, then turned toward Ursula. "It was a pleasure meeting you, Mrs. Bentz."

"Let me see you to the door, Doctor."

The hairs at the nape of Katie's neck rose as Josh took a step toward her, then paused. "I'll see you back at the house, Katie."

She nodded. The clipped sound of his boots moving away from her caused a knot to lodge in her chest. She paced to the opposite corner. It had only been a kiss. A lovely kiss that had made her toes curl and her heart want things she couldn't have. Like a home and a family, and a husband who could love her despite her profession.

A man like Josh.

* * *

"Sit down," Ursula begged, placing china cups with saucers on the table nearest the kitchen. "Your pacing around like that is making me nervous."

"I'm sorry." That seemed to be the only phrase Katie could say. How could she—levelheaded, sensible Katie—have acted so shamefully? What would her father say? The town council? What would happen to the students she tutored?

"Worrying about it isn't going to change things." Ursula laid out silverware along with a small pot of honey and a miniature pitcher of cream.

"I know." Katie buried her face in her hands. "I just can't believe that, after all the hard work I've done to build my reputation as a doctor, I shamed myself like that."

"Well, many a young lady has lost her head over a handsome man."

The heated scent of chamomile and mint drifting through the air as Ursula filled a cup took a faint edge off Katie's raw feelings. "I never have."

"There's always a first time, Katie."

And what a lovely first kiss it had been! Katie touched her fingers to her mouth, her lips tingling at the thought of Josh's head bending toward hers, the firm, warm brush of his lips against hers. What would it be like to look over the dinner table at him every night, to share their hopes and dreams over a chess match? To wake up every morning next to her best friend. A little sigh escaped her.

"Daydreaming?"

Katie blinked. "A little."

"Maybe you shouldn't wait. Saint Valentine's Day is in a few days. You could plan to exchange your vows then."

If only it were that easy. But Josh was here to break the marriage contract, not go through with it. And in truth, she wouldn't go through with it either, not unless it was for all the right reasons. Such as love and respect. Shaking her head, Katie reached for the pitcher of cream and poured a sizable portion in her tea. "Valentine's Day won't work."

Ursula clasped a cool hand over Katie's forearm. "If you're worried about your papa, have the wedding at his bedside. He won't care as long as he's there and you're happy."

Her friend was right. If Papa thought marrying Josh would make her happy, he'd do anything to make it possible, even invoking that horrible marriage agreement. Katie lifted the cup to her lips. "It's a bit more complicated than that."

Ursula's cup clinked softly against the china saucer. "I don't understand."

Best just to be truthful. "Josh and I aren't getting married."

"So Dr. McClain lied to us?"

"No." She shook her head. "He was correct in telling you that we are betrothed. It's just…our fathers signed a contract years ago, promising us to each other without our knowledge."

"Oh," Ursula said, leaning back in her chair. "So you don't know this man?"

"No— I mean, yes, I know him. Very well, in fact. He was my closest friend for many years."

A tiny line of confusion formed between her friend's eyes. "But you don't like him anymore. He became a bad man?"

Katie shook her head. "Josh isn't bad. He's very good,

very kind and encouraging, everything a girl could want in the man she marries."

Ursula's face softened, and her mouth lifted in a faint smile. "Then why won't you marry him?"

"I would, if I thought he wanted me." She straightened her shoulders, amazed that her trembling hand hadn't sloshed hot tea all over Ursula's lace tablecloth. "But he's been very honest about it. He wants to break the contract so he can leave and set up a new practice in Kansas."

"Plans change."

"I don't think his plans will." But, oh, how Katie wished they would. But Josh had the right to choose his own bride, not an old friend foisted on him by their families. He deserved a wife who could give him all the comforts, who would fit into the society he would probably one day return to in Charleston. "Josh doesn't want to marry me."

"Oh, Katie, Miss Whipple was very clear. If you're not married within the next month, she intends to go to the board at Hillsdale and tell them what she saw today. She could close down our boardinghouse."

"Papa wouldn't let them do that." But if Principal Whipple was that determined to close the boardinghouse, what would she do to Papa? Recommend that he be fired from his teaching position? They wouldn't be able to take care of their patients.

"Are you so sure Dr. McClain doesn't want to marry you?"

Katie nodded. "He came to Hillsdale just to break the contract."

"But what if he's changed his mind? I mean, I saw the two of you."

Heat rose in Katie's cheeks. "He just kissed me to teach me a lesson."

"I wasn't talking about that, but there is that to consider." Ursula took another sip. "Men are very protective creatures, particularly where their loved ones are concerned."

"Of course Josh would protect me." He'd spent their entire childhood protecting her. But, she admitted to herself, it had felt different since he arrived, more intimate than in the past, almost as if he were staking a claim.

Or was it just wishful thinking?

Putting down her cup, Katie rested her head in one warm hand. "I can't let you lose your business because of me."

"Things will work out." A soothing hand stroked her back before coming to rest on her shoulder. "We'll get through this, just like we do everything else. Taking our worries to God. Giving ourselves over to His will."

And if it was God's will that Ursula and Josef lose their income? And her father, his position? Not to mention for her to lose Josh and their relationship? She'd cross that bridge when she came to it. "Would you pray with me?"

Ursula nodded. "Yes, and let's remember Liberty in our prayers, too."

"Why?" Katie lifted her head to study her friend's face. "Is something wrong?"

"No, it's just that…" Ursula hesitated, bending closer as if expecting the walls to grow ears. "Yesterday, she was with me in the kitchen when this young man came to the back door. He said he was sorry for hurting her."

"What had he done?"

"I'm not sure, but she was flustered. She seemed to

feel differently about him than the young men who usually court her."

That was strange, given how particular Liberty was about men. "Was he involved in the train wreck?"

Ursula nodded. "And Liberty seemed to know him. Maybe he's somcone she knows from Chicago."

There was only one man Liberty had ever mentioned to Katie, an architect who was best friends with her older brother, but he had been traveling in Europe for over a year. It couldn't be....

But then, she'd thought she'd never see Josh again, and look what had happened. Everyone in town would soon think they were engaged.

Ursula chuckled softly beside her. "What's so funny?"

"I was just thinking. Cupid must have been riding along on the South Michigan the other night."

Chapter 8

Josh balled up the sheet of paper and flung it into the fire, his fifth attempt at making a list of supplies and equipment since coming back to the Clarks'. He'd been relieved when Katie had stayed behind to talk to her friend Ursula. He needed time to think, to sort through the mess he'd created since arriving in Hillsdale. But his thoughts always strayed back to Katie.

He stood; the restless irritation he'd been feeling since leaving the boardinghouse seemed to build up inside him. Walking over to the fireplace, he rested his hands on the mantel, his boot perched on the hearth as he stared down in the glowing embers. The nerve of Miss Whipple! The dressing-down that woman had given Katie with just a glance had set his teeth on edge. How dare she lecture Katie about being an acceptable role model for respectable young ladies! Didn't she realize what Katie had accomplished, not only for herself, but for every lady with a dream of attending college, of going into a profession? Why, the principal should be championing Katie's cause, not condemning her. And why all the fuss over a friendly little kiss?

Only there hadn't been anything friendly about it.

His gut tightened. He'd expected her to laugh, maybe even give him a playful punch on the shoulder like she used to whenever his teasing got out of hand. But when she'd tilted her head back, exposing the graceful line of her jaw, the tiny wisps of curls that framed her face, the thick lashes that outlined those lovely coffee-colored eyes of hers, his brain had muddled. This was Katie, his Katie. In that moment, from one heartbeat to the next, he'd realized how dangerously close he was to falling in love with her.

But what about the plans I've made, Lord? Where does Katie fit into all those?

Pushing away from the fireplace, Josh walked back over to the secretary and sat down, stretching his legs out in front of him, arms crossed over his chest. Did it really matter anyway? Kate had already informed him in that impossibly blunt way of hers that she wouldn't marry him.

But if he was on the path God had planned for him, why did Josh feel this restlessness, this uncertainty in his soul?

There was a knock on the door. "Dr. McClain?"

Josh straightened, picking up the scattered papers on the desk and stacking them into a neat little pile. "What is it, Ada?"

"Dr. Clark would like to speak with you."

Katie was home? He hadn't heard her come in. But

then, Katie wouldn't have thought anything of disturbing him in her own parlor. "You mean the older Dr. Clark."

The woman looked confused for a moment, then nodded. "Yes, sir."

Josh stood, hooking his suit coat off the back of his chair, then throwing it back down. No sense putting it on when he needed to check the man's wound. "Is he in distress?"

She shook her head. "No, just said he needed to talk to you without Dr. Katie around."

Josh tugged down the sleeves of his shirt. Both he and Katie had agreed there'd be time to discuss the marriage contract with her father later, once he'd had a few days to heal. So, what was so important that the older man needed to speak to him privately? "Tell him I'll be right there."

"Yes, sir." The young woman nodded her head in a quick bow, then left as unobtrusively as she had come.

Josh fiddled with the buttons on his vest as he headed across the hall and up the stairs, finally threading the last one into place as he stood in front of Dr. Clark's door. With a deep breath, he lifted his fist and knocked.

"Come in."

The brass doorknob turned easily in Josh's hand, and he pushed the door open. The room looked different, brighter. A stack of books rested on a bedside table well within the doctor's reach along with a clean handkerchief and a glass of water. The faded white linens had been replaced with crisp snowy ones that made the splashes of the forest-green and sky-blues in the plush quilt on the bed burst into color. In the center of the bed, Dr. Clark lay propped up, pillows layered behind him and down the length of his injured leg.

Katie might have made some suggestions, but she'd been too busy to orchestrate this. "It looks as though Mrs. Holden has been busy."

A faint flush of color rose in the older man's cheeks as he seemed to sink lower into the pillows. "I'd forgotten how nice it is to have a woman buzzing around you. There's something downright comforting about it."

"Particularly if it's the right lady, I'm sure," Josh answered, unbuttoning his shirtsleeves and pushing them up his arms. The image of Katie making a home with him, building a practice together, floated through his thoughts. He washed his hands quickly, then turned back to his patient. "Mind if I check your wound?"

"No, go right ahead," the older man answered, laying his book aside. "How are you doing? Hands giving you any trouble today?"

Josh gathered a roll of fresh bandages and several towels from the chest of drawers and walked over to the bed. "Not really. That ointment Katie used took the sting out of the burns."

"Katie came up with that mixture herself." Clark pushed himself up higher on his pillows as if he intended to watch Josh work.

"Every time I've heard her ask for it, it's always your ointment."

"Yes, well." He grimaced, though from pain or something else, Josh couldn't be sure. "It's just easier than trying to defend Katie's abilities to a town of doubting Thomases." He hesitated for a moment. "How is Katie really doing? Is she taking care of herself?"

The note of concern jarred Josh. Unlike his own father, Josh remembered Ethan Clark always worried about his daughter. He lifted the edge of the quilt, tucking it in around the uninjured leg, giving him a clear view of the wound. "She's fine. I asked Mrs. Holden to make sure she's eating and sleeping properly."

"And the patients?"

"Better than one might expect after a train wreck, though Mrs. McDaniels is doing poorly," Josh answered, picking up a pair of scissors and clipping the soiled bandage. "Katie worked out a plan with the town council pairing up victims with folks in town. So far, we've had no complaints."

"Should've known my girl would coordinate everything so well. Nothing more than what I expected."

Josh stole a glance at him then. "So you know Katie is an excellent physician?"

"Of course I do. My daughter is better than any other doctor I've ever worked with."

Then why had he refused to advertise Katie's medical degree on his shingle in front of the house? And what about the men she tutored at the college? Why didn't she have a class of her own?

Josh peeled back the bandage, noting the pink skin. "This looks very good. No signs of infection so far."

"Good, I've still got a few things to do before I die."

Removing the bloodstained bandages, Josh picked up a towel and cleaned around the wound. "Like what?"

Clark ignored Josh's question. "You don't seem to have a problem with my Katie being a doctor."

"It's the right profession for her." Josh drew in a long breath through his nostrils, blotting carbolic acid into the wound site. "I just wish people around here could appreciate Katie for who she is instead of expecting her to be like everyone else."

The older man crossed his arms over his chest and

studied him. "I agree, son. But respect is earned with hard work, not just because you've got a piece of paper from some fancy university back East."

Maybe not, but her father's help might have given Katie the boost she needed. "How much more does she have to give to prove herself to these people? Another year? Five? The rest of her life?"

The older man eyed him. "That sounds very much like admiration to me."

"Well, certainly," Josh replied. "As one colleague to another."

"Humph." Dr. Clark's sigh echoed in the room. "Looks like that shiner's getting better. Reckon you're sore today."

"Not much. I worked out a lot of the stiffness while Katie and I did rounds this morning."

"Mrs. Holden tells me you lost everything in the fire. A couple of trunks, some boxes."

He tucked the end of the fresh bandage against Clark's leg. "Everything except for what I carried off the train with me."

"I'm so sorry, son. Is there anything we can do for you?"

Two days ago, Josh would have taken this opening and run right through it, but something held him back. Both he and Katie had agreed to wait until her father was further along in his recovery before bringing up the subject of the marriage contract, but the older doctor seemed to be healing quite well. Even Katie would agree. Why was he hesitating?

Josh shook his head. "Charlie down at the station says that the Southern Michigan will make full restitution, but it might take a week or two. Not sure if that's going to help me, though."

"Why's that?"

Josh sat down in the ladder-back chair he'd brought in for Katie earlier that morning. "I'm supposed to be in Kansas to start my new job as soon as the weather breaks." He explained how he'd been hired by a group of farmers building a new town on the outskirts of Kansas City. "But they were very clear about their time line. I have to be there and prepared to open my practice by the first week of March."

"Farmers are a stubborn bunch, the whole lot of them. But I guess that's what it takes to wrestle with the dirt and wind and weather to get a crop out of the ground." Dr. Clark chuckled softly. "You know, Katie talked about moving out West right after she graduated from medical school. I guess she thought they might be desperate enough to hire a female doctor."

Katie, in uncharted territory alone? The stories Josh had heard about the savage men, both Indian and white, had given him reason to pause, but Katie? The thought sent his heart pounding, a protectiveness stronger than anything he'd felt in their childhood friendship roaring through his blood. "You weren't going to allow her to go, were you?"

"If that was what she had wanted, then, yes, I would have."

Had the older man gone mad? Just the thought of Katie in the wildness of Kansas plunged a knife through Josh's chest. But if she'd wanted to go, there'd be no stopping her. So why didn't she follow through with her plans? "What happened?"

"Not really sure. It just seemed like all the fight went out of her one day," Clark replied, a deep line between his eyes. "It worries me sometimes."

Josh nodded. It would worry him, too. The Katie he knew wouldn't have let anyone get in her way, stubborn mite that she was. Had the constraints of a society that was frightened by the thought of a woman practicing medicine broken her spirit? Or did she just need someone who believed in her to help her begin the fight again?

"Well, son, you want to tell me why you're here?"

This change of topic caught Josh a little off guard. He leaned forward, his elbows on his knees, threading his fingers together while he gathered his thoughts. "It's about the marriage contract you and my father signed."

"And here I thought you'd finally come to see Katie." A faint smile lifted the corners of the older man's mouth. "She missed you, you know."

"She did?"

Clark nodded. "She wrote to you. It was painful for her, leaving you when you were still grieving for your mother, but she wanted you to know that she was praying for you."

Josh would have cherished that letter. "I never received it. Father had…" He couldn't say it, that Samuel McClain had broken down, despondent over his financial missteps and the loss of his wife until finally his weak grasp on reality had snapped. "Father fell ill after Mother died, and I had to learn how to handle the estate very quickly." Not that there'd been much left to handle.

"She thought as much. She only stopped writing you after she left for medical school."

She'd written numerous times? Why had he never received any of her letters? Had they been lost? Or had his father disposed of them out of fear Josh would discover his involvement in brokering the marriage contract?

And why had Kate stopped writing once she'd left for

medical school? Had she feared his response to her chosen profession—that he would react like everyone else and try to talk her out of becoming a doctor?

The door opened, and Ada ducked her head inside. "Dr. McClain? Mr. McDaniels is here to get a report on his wife."

"Tell him I'll be right there."

"Yes, sir." The door shut behind her.

Josh stood. His thoughts tumbled over each other, gathering speed as if rolling down an endless hill. "Dr. Clark, I have to ask. Why did you and my father enter into such an agreement without so much as telling either of us?"

"Go, your patient needs you." The older man sank back into his pillows, a hint of compassion in his eyes before his lids drifted down, and he fell asleep.

Katie sat on the sofa, her knees drawn up to her chest, her wrapper and night shift tucked in tightly around her bare feet. Though the fire had not yet turned to ash, there was a chill in the air that sank down into her bones. She grabbed the quilt draped across the back of the couch and spread it over her, pulling the covers up under her chin.

She leaned her head back into the cushions, her limbs heavy, her muscles aching for the release only sleep would give. But her mind whirled, one thought chasing after another. It had been like this for the past two nights, since that stolen kiss with Josh. She didn't regret what had happened, but had decided it would be best to avoid him as much as she could.

An almost impossible task with him staying under the same roof. Over the breakfast table in the mornings, meeting him in the hallway as she headed out for rounds.

And last night, he'd been visiting with Papa when she'd gone in to say good-night. She missed Josh. This was not the dull ache she'd felt over the years after she'd left South Carolina. No, this pain cut straight through her, stung her heart with the sharpness of the most well-hewed blade.

"Couldn't sleep?"

Katie lifted her head to find Mrs. Holden in the doorway. "Have a lot on my mind. Is Papa…?"

"He's fine, just asked for a glass of warm milk. You want me to make some for you? Might help."

Katie nodded. "Thank you."

The soft rustle of Mrs. Holden's skirts faded as Katie laid her head back. The woman was perfect for her father—warm, caring, but still her own person. She had a way of drawing Papa out of his usual serious self, earning a smile or a bark of laughter that never failed to surprise Katie. So, why had he never offered for Mrs. Holden? Was he so worried about Katie that he'd put his own happiness on the shelf? She closed her eyes. *Oh, Lord, Papa deserves to be happy instead of fretting about me.*

Her thoughts drifted and scattered. *When will I find my way?*

"I thought you'd be asleep."

Katie's eyes flew open, her heart thumping against her ribs as she turned to find Josh standing in the doorway. A swatch of hair hung down over his forehead, his blond hair sticking out at different angles in a rumpled mess that made her fingers itch to comb it into place. His vest hung open, his shirtsleeves rolled up over his forearms as if he'd just come from a patient's bedside. "Checking on Mrs. McDaniels?"

His shoulders slumped slightly as he walked over to the couch. The cushions moved beneath her as he sat down. "She's hung on longer than I would have expected."

Katie huddled into her blankets. "Maybe she just needs time to say her goodbyes."

He sat back, one arm wrapping tightly around his midsection while he rubbed his chin in his free hand. "You think Mr. McDaniels understands that?"

"I don't know. But maybe, in the years to come, he can remember it for what it truly is, a chance to say goodbye."

Josh drew in a deep sigh. "Father never understood that, you know, when Mother died. He'd been too busy trying to find a way to save her."

"And you?"

"I knew it was a lost cause."

He stared into the fire, the yellowish-gold light dancing across his features: the tiny knot in his nose where he'd broken it saving another one of her animals from the oak in the front yard, the lush lashes that framed blue eyes, the tiny scar under his lower lip. Yes, she found him attractive, but it was the man he'd become, the one she'd only seen glimpses of in her childhood, that held her heart.

"It must have been harder for you. You didn't even get to say goodbye to your mother."

"No, Mama died almost instantly." But Katie hadn't needed a long goodbye to know what her mother felt for her. She'd known it every time Mama had complained about losing her figure, in her hurtful remarks about Katie's mousy brown hair and her tomboy ways. "It was for the best."

"I remember your mother." Crossing his ankle over one knee, Josh stretched his arm along the back of the sofa, causing a flutter in Katie's midsection. "A very particular lady."

The description startled Katie. "I beg your pardon."

"You know I don't mean any harm, but your mother seemed more committed to making you more like her instead of allowing you to grow into your own person."

That remark hit too close to the mark. "You mean like your father molded you to take over his businesses?"

She expected Josh to rail, as he had in the past when she mentioned his father's tight hold on him. But this time, he chuckled. "Looks like neither one of them succeeded very well."

He was right. Neither of them had turned out exactly as their parents had hoped. "Why did you become a doctor?"

"You're probably going to laugh at me."

"I will not."

Josh glanced over at her. "You."

"Me? I wasn't even around when you made the decision to study medicine."

He ducked his head slightly but not before she caught his faint smile. "No, but the memory of you doctoring all those animals stayed with me. The way you almost glowed when one would recover."

"I lost a lot of those animals, too." She'd cried her eyes out each time. But Josh had never left her alone, always holding her until she'd been ready to move forward. "Don't you remember that?"

"I know. You hurt for them because they mattered. You made a difference. I wanted to make a difference, too." He hesitated for a moment. "So I began praying for God to give me a sign, anything to let me know I was on the right path."

Katie smiled. "You were laying out your fleece."

"A few weeks later, there was an outbreak of fever at the college. It was over relatively fast and no one died, thank God, but I had my answer."

"Poor man," Katie answered with a chuckle. "How did your father handle it?"

"Not good at first. He threatened to cut me off."

Katie seriously doubted that. Josh had always been the pride and joy of Samuel McClain's life. "Are you telling me another fairy tale? Because I knew your father, and he wouldn't have done that."

"I never could pull anything on you, could I?" He gave her a sheepish grin. "Father wasn't much use to anyone right after Mother passed. He blamed himself for not securing them a driver. He blamed our steward for giving my mother the reins. He even blamed me for a while. So at the time, he didn't really care what I did as long as I stayed out of his sight."

"People do that when they're grieving," she replied. But the knowledge couldn't have made it any easier for him.

"I know that now. But then, I think I was as lost as Father was. Everything around me changed so much. Mother was gone. Father couldn't put two sentences together because of the spirits."

"You were alone." Just like Katie had been in those mind-numbing days after her mother had died. Each moment, each second had brought a fresh wave of pain. But even then, Josh had been there, saying comforting words, gently forcing her to eat and rest as he had that first morning after the crash. No wonder he came to break the wedding contract.

The quilt fell away as she reached out one hand and covered his. "I'm sorry I wasn't there for you."

He captured her fingers in his. "Your father tells me that you wrote."

"You didn't receive them?"

He shook his head. "How many were there?"

She pulled her hand back under the blanket. "Just a few." A few dozen, one every week until she realized he didn't care enough to write her back.

"I wish I had received them, Katie."

She nodded, drawing herself up against the corner of the couch. She'd poured her heart into those letters, the mixed emotions she'd felt about her mother's death, because Josh understood her. He always had and, she suspected, always would.

Josh shifted back into the cushions. "You know, I'm glad God made it easy for me to figure out that He wanted me to be a doctor. I'd hate to think of all the plagues Charleston would have endured if I'd been the least bit thick-skulled."

"Don't tease about that. You were open to listening to the Lord's will for your life."

The teasing in Josh's eyes suddenly evaporated, replaced by a puzzling curiosity that made him study her intently. She felt a gentle tug to her braid and glanced down, her breath catching as the loose ends curled around his finger.

Josh dropped his hand and leaned back. "I've missed you these last couple of days."

"What about the seven years before that?" Katie teased. She needed to keep things light and airy between them, not explore emotions that felt too sharp and vivid to escape with her heart intact. But now that the question was out there, she very much wanted an answer.

"I missed you then, too. I just didn't know it."

It was on the tip of her tongue to ask him what he meant when Mrs. Holden rushed in, gasping for air. "Come quick. It's Mrs. McDaniels."

They both jumped up in unison, Katie tossing the quilt on the couch, then shoving her stocking feet into slippers, tightening the thick cords of her wrapper as she followed Josh and Mrs. Holden into the hallway.

Hurrying to the coatrack, Josh reached for his hat. "I'll go and get McDaniels."

"I don't know if that's a good idea, Josh. You know how he feels about me taking care of his wife."

Josh pushed his arm into one sleeve of his wool coat, then the other. "We've done everything medically possible for Mrs. McDaniels. Now it's time to leave it up to the Lord."

He was right. They'd known from the first Molly McDaniels's injuries would end in her death. All anyone could do for her now was help relieve the pain. "Go, and pray she hangs on until you get back."

Josh rushed to the door, then turned and came back to stand in front of her, his eyes full of compassion and admiration. She sucked in a shallow breath when he brushed a swift kiss against her forehead. "I'll be praying for you, too."

Katie basked in the brief moment of pure peace until the front door clicked shut, and Josh was gone.

A high-pitched wail rent the upstairs hallway. Grabbing the long skirt of her wrapper in her hands, Katie hurried toward the stairs, her pulse pounding as she took two steps at a time. She hated this part of medicine, despised the thought of a life wasted. But at least she could make Mrs. McDaniels's last moments on this earth peaceful.

The pall of death hung like a heavy velvet curtain in the small bedroom, the stifling air hot. Rushing to the window, Katie glanced to where Ada stood by the bedside, rubbing down Mrs. McDaniels's arms with a wet cloth. "Please, get another blanket for Mrs. McDaniels, and a dose of laudanum, as well. And tell Mrs. Holden to make some strong coffee."

Ada nodded, her face pale, her mouth in a grim line as she darted out the door.

Katie pushed against the window frame, her arms beginning to shake when it suddenly popped, then slid open. Frigid air bit through the thick fabric of Katie's wrapper and nightgown, and she shivered, but her comfort didn't matter, only that of Mrs. McDaniels.

Walking to the bed, Katie did a quick assessment of the woman, her stomach sinking with each piece of information she took in. Molly McDaniels lay on her side, her legs drawn up to her chest, her arm clamped tightly against her side. A faint blue tinge had replaced the ghostly white color in her face, her lips a deeper shade of purple, the skin around her eyes and mouth wrinkled with pain. She was dying, and there was nothing Katie could do.

Please, Lord, let Mr. McDaniels get here in time!

Ada came flying into the room, the quilt Katie had used earlier thrown over one shoulder, balancing a small glass in her hand. Katie took it and walked over to the bed. She leveled her arm behind the woman's shoulders and lifted her slightly. "Here you go, Mrs. McDaniels. This will help ease the pain."

"No, I...awake." The woman panted, her head rolling from side to side. "Hiram."

Katie's gut tightened. The small amount of laudanum probably wouldn't dull the woman's senses, but she'd have a hard time convincing Mrs. McDaniels. "Just a little bit, then. Enough to take the edge off so that you can talk to your husband."

With a sharp breath, the woman pressed her lips into a hard line and shook her head.

"What are we going to do?" Ada stared up, wide-eyed.

A sense of hopelessness fell over Katie. How could she give this woman comfort if she refused it? Maybe there was something else she could do, just to dull the pain. Crouching down, Katie trapped the woman's head between her hands and moved in close, their gazes meeting. "Mrs. McDaniels, I'm going to administer some ether. You'll still be able to talk to your husband because I won't give you enough to put you to sleep."

She suddenly stopped struggling.

Ada handed Katie a clean cotton cloth and a small glass bottle full of clear liquid, a faint hint of a sickening sweet odor coming from its open top. Pressing the opening to the cloth square, Katie tipped it over, making a small damp circle, then gave the bottle back to Ada. *Lord, please let this help!*

As Katie pressed the cloth over the woman's nose and mouth, the woman breathed deeply, her eyelids drooped slightly as, in the background, the sound of boots charging up the front stairs exploded through the near silence. Katie brushed fine strands of faded reddish-gold hair from the woman's face. "Hold on just a little longer, Molly. Hiram's almost here."

Chapter 9

"Molly?" Mr. McDaniels flew through the doorway, not stopping until he crumbled beside the bed, his arms reaching for his wife.

"I'm glad you're here," Molly slurred, her eyes half-shut by droopy lids. She looked peaceful, almost serene, as she stared into her husband's eyes. "We've had a good life, haven't we?"

McDaniels swallowed hard. "Yes, we have, darling. Thirty wonderful years."

Thirty years, Josh thought. A lifetime, really, full of ups and downs, good times and sadness. Watching his father fall apart, he'd thought nothing could be worth the heartache of losing the one you loved. But now he wasn't so sure.

His gaze shifted to Katie. Her braid had come unraveled, her dark hair flowing in long unruly cords over her shoulders, puddling into a wave of curls at the small of her back. Her face had lost all color, her lips pale, tiny lines worrying the area around her mouth. She had played such an important role in his childhood, his best friend. Would he rather have been alone than share the joy of those moments with her, even if it meant bearing her loss?

Katie held up a white square close to the woman's face. "Mrs. McDaniels, I need you to take another breath."

But her husband pushed Katie's hand away. "What are you doing?"

"Mr. McDaniels, your wife is in a great deal of pain." Katie spoke softly, her voice warmed by concern. "I'm administering a small dose of ether just to help her bear it."

The man looked over her shoulder to Josh. "Is that what you would do?"

Why wasn't Katie using laudanum first? Knowing her, there had to be a good reason. Josh nodded. "Yes, if I felt that was the only way to control your wife's pain, I would do the exact same thing."

The man leaned back, then nodded. Katie reached over, covering the woman's mouth and nose with the cloth. "Here, take a deep breath, Molly."

Molly breathed in, then nestled back into her husband's arm, her head pillowed against his chest. "Do you remember when we met?"

Hiram chuckled, a stray tear running down his face. "I'd gotten in trouble with Old Man Larson. He told my daddy that he'd forgive me if I went to church for a month. I wasn't too keen on it, until I walked in that door and saw you sitting there, your hair hanging down your back in ribbons. I don't think I missed another Sunday until after we lost Jeremy."

Molly's face took on an unearthly glow. "I'll get to see him soon."

"Yes, you will, my love." He gathered his wife closer to him, burying his face in the long strands of her reddish-gold hair.

A verse teased along the edges of Josh's memory. *For in everything there is a season, a time to be born and a time to die.*

This was Hiram McDaniels's time to mourn. Josh walked over to where Katie stood and slipped his hand under her elbow. "Let's give them some time alone."

She nodded, moisture glistening in the dark fringe of lashes. "Mr. McDaniels, we'll be just outside if you should need us."

He didn't respond, just held his wife closer as if sheer will could hold her in this world. Poor man. He was still relatively young, about the age of Josh's father when his mother had passed. Maybe with some time, he could move on, be happy again. Or would McDaniels end up like Josh's father? What was it Father had said after a particularly rough night? How did you recover when you'd lost the best part of yourself this side of heaven? The heart of your home?

But what was worse, to have found and lost the love of a lifetime, or to never have found love at all?

Following Katie out into the dimly lit hall, he couldn't help wondering what it would be like to wake up beside Katie every morning, watch her grow into the doctor, the woman, God wanted her to be, hold her in his arms as they passed through this life into the next.

Katie collapsed with her back against the wall, her hands braced on her knees. "I knew it was going to happen. We all did, but..." Her voice caught. She swallowed, then straightened. "I hate feeling so useless."

His first instinct was to reach out, to pull her into his arms and hold her close, just as he had done when he'd comforted her after losing one of her animal patients. But this Katie was a grown woman, a physician, frustrated by the loss of her patient, dissecting the events, trying to figure out what she could have done differently. How she could have saved a life.

Josh leaned back against the wall next to her. "Tell me what happened."

Katie gave a very detailed description of Mrs. McDaniels's appearance, suggesting possible treatments, invalidating them as she continued to speak. He'd always known Katie had a gift of healing, but her commonsense approach and logical thinking was what made her a great doctor.

When she finally got through every conceivable possibility, she sighed. "There was nothing else to be done."

"It's been a matter of time with Mrs. McDaniels ever since the wreck."

"I know." She dropped her chin to her chest, her shoulders rounded. "I'm just glad you got here with Mr. McDaniels when you did. She so wanted to see him one last time."

Josh reached down and covered her hand with his. "It's their time."

"To every thing, there is a season." She breathed, tilting her head slightly to look up at him, a faint smile on her lips. "Those verses in Ecclesiastes 2 are what I cling to whenever I lose a patient."

"It still doesn't make losing someone easy."

Katie squeezed his fingers. "No, but it makes these moments easier to bear."

"I don't see how."

Katie turned, leaning one shoulder against the wall. "Do you remember studying Newton's law about equal yet opposite reactions?"

Josh wasn't quite sure where she was leading with this, but he was willing to hear her out. "Yes."

"In those verses, we see the truth of this. A time to be born and a time to die. A time to weep and a time to laugh."

"A time to love and a time to hate."

She gave him a faint smile. "Remembering that truth is what helps me through the bad times."

Josh leaned his head back. Was that what he'd been doing, focusing so much on the hardships, the loss, that he'd refused to open himself up to the joy that was standing right in front of him? Losing Katie the first time had been difficult, but was letting himself fall in love with her worth the risk?

"Katie, is everything all right?"

"Papa! What are you doing out of bed?" Katie pushed off the wall and hurried toward the man leaning against the door frame. "You know better than that."

"Josh told me I should move around a bit, get my blood pumping."

She cast him a questioning glance. "Is that true?"

"Yes, ma'am."

Katie didn't look convinced. Wrapping her arm around her father's waist, she took his hand in hers. "Then tomorrow we can take a stroll down the hall, but tonight it's late and you need your sleep."

"All this fuss," the older man muttered, but there was

a loving glint in his eyes. "What you need is a house full of children to take care of."

Her cheeks flushed a deep red as she waited for her father to turn around. "In case you haven't noticed, I'd need a husband for that."

Clark glanced over at Josh. "Well, you know Rand would be most obliging."

The door clicked shut before Josh could hear Katie's reply. Rand Dawes! What on earth could Katie see in the man? He was passably nice, Josh supposed, and, being the sheriff, knew how to handle himself in most every given situation. But marriage was more than those things. Would he challenge her quick intellect on those evenings at home by the fireplace? Or would he force her to turn into someone she wasn't, killing her independent spirit, taking his Katie from him?

He was so deep in thought, he didn't hear the door open. "Dr. McClain?"

The expression on Ada's face as she stood in the doorway told him everything he needed to know.

Molly McDaniels was gone.

Over the next few hours, Josh kept vigil with Mr. McDaniels, listening to his stories of his life with Mrs. McDaniels: their first meeting at church, their wedding in that same church three years later, leaving their family in Ireland behind, hoping for a new start with their children in Boston. Thirty years of love and joy, of good times and bad, children and grandchildren. Growing together, becoming one as God intended.

In the darkest hours of the early morning, listening to McDaniels tell yet another story, Josh realized the truth. He loved Katie, loved her so much that the thought of living without her caused an ache deep in his soul. She'd always been his better half, the heart to his home, only he'd been too young to see it then. If Katie had stayed in Charleston, if they'd had the opportunity to work through the awkwardness of youth, would they have been married by now? Have children of their own?

Thank You, Lord, for making our fathers draw up that marriage contract! Without it, Josh would never have made the trip to Hillsdale, never reclaimed all the memories they shared, never realized that Katie had always been the only one he could trust with his heart.

But could he win her heart? Katie didn't want to marry him—she'd told him that much—but that had been when she'd first learned about the agreement between their fathers. Could he convince her to marry him for love rather than some medieval scheme their parents had conjured up?

The candles had burned themselves out by the time McDaniels finally nodded off. Josh couldn't leave him alone, not in case the man woke up, so he burrowed down into a straight-backed chair, crossed his arms over his chest and closed his eyes. Sleep came in fitful spurts, dreamless with thoughts of Katie waking him through what was left of the dark.

When Josh forced his eyelids open, the muted light coming in through the window had painted the room a somber blue-gray. These rooms grew bitterly cold at night, but he felt comfortable, warm from the quilt that had been draped over him sometime during the night. One glance at McDaniels confirmed he still slept, his upper body sprawled on the mattress, a blanket neatly tucked in around him. Who had checked on them in the night?

Josh took a breath of cold air, a hint of lavender teasing him with its feminine scent. Katie. She'd be starting rounds early this morning, particularly if she wanted to make it to church on time. He aimed to tag along. The more time with Katie, the better to make his case for her heart. But he couldn't leave McDaniels alone just yet. Grief drove people to do strange things. Maybe they could stop by Ursula's while they were out and enlist help among Dr. Clark's students to watch McDaniels until his family could arrive from Chicago.

I need to get a move on. Josh straightened, his muscles and joints voicing their disapproval of his sleeping arrangements. Well, walking around town with Katie would soothe the aches and pains. He moved slowly toward the door. McDaniels would do better with more rest. The hinges on the door groaned softly as he opened it and stepped out into the hall.

The soft rustle of skirts whispered behind him as Josh felt the knob click into place and turn. After a night of stark mourning, the thought of seeing Katie made him feel alive and energetic, as if he could take on the world as long as she was a part of it.

"What is it?" she whispered. How could she have sensed a difference in him when he'd just realized it himself?

There wasn't time to ask. Josh slipped his hand under her elbow, enjoying the feel of the delicate bones beneath her sleeve. He led her down the hallway to the top of the stairs before he spoke. "Thank you for the blankets."

She lowered her gaze to study the step. "It can get cold at night. I just couldn't stand the thought of you two shivering to death."

Her slight cringe at her choice of words didn't escape him. "I appreciate the thought."

Katie looked past his shoulder toward Molly's door. "How is he doing?"

"About as well as can be expected. Later this afternoon, I'm going to see if Charlie can open up the telegraph office so I can send a message to his daughter in Chicago."

"I'd hate to have to send that telegram."

Josh nodded. "Their daughter has to be worried. They were headed there to see their new grandson when the accident happened."

Katie mashed her lips together, a telling expression Josh recognized from their youth. Despite Mr. McDaniels's behavior toward her earlier, she hurt for him. That was the kind of woman Katie was, one of the reasons he loved her.

The moment passed. "How are you?"

Josh stretched to one side. "Nothing a little walk around town won't take care of."

"You think I'm going to let you help me on rounds after you've been up all night?" Katie shook her head. "I don't think so."

"I wouldn't be able to sleep." That was the truth, not when all he wanted in the world was to be near her, to convince her they had a future together, that he loved her.

The feel of her cool fingers along his unshaven jaw surprised him into silence. Her thumb gently scraped along the edges of his sutured cut. "That eye is looking better. The stitches will need to come out soon."

The concern behind her words gave Josh hope. "I have a very good doctor."

The shy smile she gave him was almost his undoing. "Then listen to your doctor. You're exhausted. Rest for a little while, then I'll come back by and we'll go to church."

Josh didn't like giving in, but the thought of worshipping with Katie was just too much to resist. "I don't like the idea of you out on the streets by yourself."

She dropped her hand to her side. "I've been doing this for quite some time on my own."

"But that doesn't mean it's a good idea."

After a long second, Katie sighed. "What if I get Mrs. Holden to go with me?"

Two women going on rounds was a sight better than Katie heading off by herself. It should satisfy him, but he knew how Katie's mind worked. "You won't be sending her home halfway through rounds, will you?"

The petulant look on her face almost made him laugh. "You don't want breakfast before church? If Mrs. Holden is with me, you won't get anything to eat."

"Don't worry. I'll take care of that," he said.

"You cook?"

"Probably not to the extent Mrs. Holden does, but I can scramble eggs." He chuckled, taking her arm and leading her the rest of the way down the stairs. "Now go, so you'll be back in time to freshen up and eat before church starts."

A quick intake of breath forced his attention to the head of the stairs, where Hiram McDaniels stood, glowering down at them.

He pointed an accusing finger at Katie. "You killed my darling Molly!"

"Are you sure you're all right, dear?" Mrs. Holden asked, giving Katie a worried look from under the brim of her bonnet.

"I'm fine. Rounds are just taking longer than I expected this morning, that's all." Of course, it hadn't helped that Katie found it necessary to change every bandage, examine every bump and bruise, nurse every cup of coffee along the way.

Mr. McDaniels's accusation had frightened her. Not the words—the man had just suffered the greatest loss of his life—but his belief in their truth. There had been a desperation about him, as if his indictment this morning wasn't the final word on the subject.

Despite her fur-lined cape, Katie shivered.

"I hate to see you like this, not when we both know that woman was blessed to have you taking care of her."

Katie wasn't sure what to say. Mrs. Holden almost sounded as if she was proud of her. "You don't agree with Mr. McDaniels that I shouldn't have been caring for her?"

"Of course not!" The older woman turned and glared at her. "Don't you know what a wonderful doctor you are?"

She shook her head, clasping her medical bag to her chest. "Well, yes, I guess."

A gloved hand lifted her chin until she was staring into Mrs. Holden's warm, golden-brown eyes. "Kathleen Clark, you know your father well enough to know he doesn't let just anyone near his patients."

That was true. Papa had a reputation around campus of being hard on his students, even stricter with her, allowing only the best to assist him. "I know."

"But he trusts your skills and your training. He's so proud of what you've accomplished, Katie." She gave Katie a motherly smile. "And though I have no right, I'm proud of you, too."

Even in the dismal cold, a ray of sunlight danced

through Katie, lifting her up, giving her a reason to hope. She leaned forward and pressed a kiss against the woman's cool cheek. "Thank you, Mrs.…Marianne."

If it was possible, the older woman's smile bloomed even wider. She latched her arm in Katie's and brought her close to her side, unlike anything her mother had ever done. "Ursula's is just around the corner. Why don't we stop in for a moment and get a cup of coffee, maybe warm up a bit?"

"Yes." It might do her some good, being among friendly faces like Ursula and Josef, and maybe even Liberty, if she hadn't left for church yet. Even if she had, Katie needed some time to collect herself before going home and facing Mr. McDaniels again.

Though the blizzard had left snowdrifts almost up to Katie's waist, foot and sleigh traffic had edged out passable trails along the sidewalks and main roads, which were brimming with people making their way to the church. A young man Katie didn't recognize paced along the sidewalk in front of the boardinghouse, clapping his gloved hands together in an effort to keep warm, occasionally tilting his hat to no one in particular.

"Must be getting up the nerve to call on a young lady," Marianne whispered.

"Must be," Katie replied, glancing at the man for a moment, taking in the expensive cut of his coat and the fine craftsmanship that went into his boots. Could this be Liberty's mystery beau that Ursula had told her about?

Marianne unlatched the gate, holding it open for Katie, who hurried up the stone walkway and stepped up onto the porch, stomping her numb feet against the floor to knock the snow off her worn boots. Then, without bothering to knock, Katie turned the knob and opened the door.

The hallway was a vibrant whirl of activity, hats and gloves flying, young ladies vying for one last moment in front of the mirror, pinning a loose curl or retying a bow just so, while the young men stood in the dining hall's doorway, peeking over their Bibles, smiling at the women's activity.

Katie relaxed just a bit. Everything about Ursula's boardinghouse spoke of life being lived, futures planned, hopes born. The doctor in her appreciated those organic activities, the natural movement of living organisms at their prime. A true example of Newton's law she and Josh had spoken of just hours before. The opposite, yet equal of her home at this moment.

"Katie!" The cry from above made her lift her gaze toward the stairs where Liberty stood, her eyes wide with worry. Grabbing up her delicate blue silk skirts, she careened down the stairs, her hem lifting to give an indecent glimpse of her stockinged calves.

Katie smiled. No one on campus quite knew what to make of Liberty. The daughter of the wealthy Judds of Chicago, her friend had shocked her parents by applying to Hillsdale College instead of putting herself out on the marriage mart, and Katie was forever thankful. Full of light and life, Liberty clung to her faith in a way that had made Katie stretch her own. And though only two years separated them, Katie felt decidedly older, giving Liberty much-needed advice and an ear to vent her frustrations with her parents.

"I've been so worried about you." Liberty threw her arms around Katie and held her close, squeezing the very breath out of her lungs. "Dr. McClain was sure you'd be here before now."

Katie pushed away. "Josh was here?"

"He told us about what happened. I'm so sorry."

"So am I. Mr. McDaniels is taking this very hard."

"Dr. McClain told us." Liberty reached for the ribbons of her bonnet and untied them. "Rand went by to check on your father this morning after you left and heard what was going on. He's staying with Mr. McDaniels while Dr. McClain rounds up some volunteers to help, and he talked to Charlie about sending a telegram to the McDaniels's daughter in Chicago."

Every nerve ending in Katie's body tingled with dread. "Josh is hopeful Mr. McDaniels's son-in-law will come and accompany him to Chicago. We're just not sure when that will be."

"Charlie said the trains will be running from that direction by Tuesday at the latest." She lifted Katie's bonnet from her head and hung it on a nearby peg. "Where will Mr. McDaniels stay while he waits for his son-in-law?"

"Well, he can't stay at the house," Marianne said. "Not with him treating Katie like that."

"We can't just toss him out, Marianne. The man's mourning his wife." Katie shook her head. "That would be cruel."

"But what about you? I couldn't bear if something..." The older woman's voice trailed off, and there was no mistaking the worry in her eyes.

Papa really should marry this woman, Katie thought, *and soon.*

"I don't think you're going to have to worry about his harming Katie," Liberty replied. "Dr. McClain was pretty adamant that Mr. McDaniels be transferred back to his room at Dr. Etheridge's home until the train is up and running again."

It was worse than she'd thought. Josh wouldn't go to

all that trouble unless he felt McDaniels posed a danger to her. Was that why he'd almost demanded to go with her on rounds this morning, because he feared for her safety? And here she'd thought he'd truly wanted to spend time with her. Her heart wept with disappointment.

While Marianne went to the kitchen to see Ursula, Katie let Liberty lead her through the maze of tables in the empty dining hall to the stone-hearth fireplace. The smoky scent of hardwoods burning in the fireplace reminded her of that first morning here with Josh. She smiled at the memory. As if she didn't know he wanted to scare her. That was why she hadn't backed down. She trusted Josh. He wouldn't hurt her. And then he'd kissed her, and her tidy little world had careened out of control.

She loved him, not with that girlish affection that had just been beginning to bloom when her father had brought her to Hillsdale, but with a stronger, deeper love—a foundation to build a life upon.

But Josh had plans. Kansas and his new practice. And he didn't want to marry her. He'd told her so. *How is this all going to work out, Lord?*

Liberty pulled two chairs out and set them in front of the fireplace. "You're concerned about Mr. McDaniels?"

"It just doesn't seem right what we're doing to him. Shouldn't we be reaching out with Christian fellowship rather than casting him out like that?" Katie absentmindedly unbuttoned her cape and let it fall from her shoulders.

"Dr. McClain said the man sounded threatening."

"He'd just lost his wife. He was beside himself with grief."

The wood popped and crackled in the long moments of silence that followed. Finally, Liberty turned. "If you feel that strongly about it, why don't you just stay here with me? It will give me a chance to finish up your dress for the Valentine's Day social."

So Liberty didn't know Katie had been barred from the boardinghouse. She slumped down in the chair. "I'd forgotten all about the social. Are you sure it's still on with everything that's happened in the last few days?"

"It's to be a celebration of life, according to Principal Whipple." She studied Katie with girlish anticipation.

"Oh. Well, I appreciate your offer, but I can't accept it." Katie hesitated, heat creeping up her neck and ears. "Principal Whipple has banned me from the boardinghouse."

"When did this happen?"

"A couple of days ago."

"Why?"

Katie pressed her hands against the raging fire in her cheeks. A woman's first kiss was special, personal, not something to be discussed and dissected even among good friends.

"Does it concern Dr. McClain?"

Katie's head snapped up. "Why would you think that?"

"He seemed very concerned for you." Liberty spoke softly. "Very attentive to your needs, almost as if he has feelings for you."

"Josh has always been very protective of me."

"So, you know him?"

"Yes." Katie briefly told her about their friendship, how they'd bonded over a love of nature and books, the awkwardness of their adolescent years, the tragic carriage accident that had claimed both their mothers. Everything but that horrid marriage contract. She was already embarrassed enough as it was.

"Then it certainly would be better for you to stay here than go back home. Besides, what Principal Whipple doesn't know won't hurt her," Liberty said.

Katie shook her head. "I won't risk getting you expelled from school."

"But, Katie…"

"It's settled. I need to be at home in case Papa needs me while he's recovering and any patients need a doctor."

Her friend didn't look too happy with her decision, but she seemed to accept it. "Is there anything I can do?"

"Pray. For me, for Josh," Katie said. "I'm not sure what to even ask for, but we need the Lord's help."

"Oh, Katie." Liberty reached up and pushed a loose strand of hair out of her face. "I always pray for you."

Katie leaned her head against her friend's shoulder, a stillness settling over her soul as Liberty spoke to the Lord on her behalf. *And, Lord, whatever happens between me and Josh, thank You for bringing him back into my life.*

Chapter 10

Josh poured himself another cup of Ms. Holden's coffee and retreated to the kitchen table, pulling out a chair. A muscle spasm cut across his lower back and down his leg. On second thought, maybe a stroll around the kitchen would work out the kinks after another night of sitting up, this time posted outside McDaniels's door. He'd hoped to have McDaniels moved before Katie returned home from rounds yesterday.

Then Katie had thrown an unexpected curve into those plans. Mr. McDaniels would stay with the Clarks until his family arrived. It was the Christian thing to do.

He had tried to reason with her, but she wouldn't be swayed. Josh kneaded his fingers into the aching muscles of his neck. Katie hadn't heard the threats the man had made against her. Josh's gut turned at the memory. Neither he nor the sheriff thought McDaniels would act on them, but stranger things had happened, and Josh wasn't about to risk Katie's safety on a hunch.

Please, Lord, keep my Katie safe.

A blast of cold air blew through the kitchen as the door swung open, the glass panes clinking like a baby's rattle. The faint musky scent of wild animals filled the room when Mr. Woods stepped inside, the coonskin hat on his head a perfect match to his own silvery-brown hair, his thick arms full of seasoned wood.

Mrs. Holden followed, slamming the door shut behind them. "You want a cup of coffee, Woody? Warm you right up on a morning like this."

Woods dropped down on one knee beside the stove and began making a neat line of wood along the base of the wall, then repeating the process until he had a perfect stack. He stood and turned, his crooked smile splitting through his scraggly beard. "Aw, Mrs. Holden, it's a rare woman who can make as fine a cup of coffee as you do."

"I have to agree with you there, Mr. Woods," Josh added, lifting his mug in agreement. "Dr. Clark is a very blessed man to have found you, Mrs. Holden."

Her cheeks turned a rose-petal pink as she turned to retrieve another cup from the cabinet. "How's our girl this morning?"

Our girl. There was a maternal possessiveness in those two words, a deep love. Clark should have married this woman years ago, when Katie needed a mother who believed in her, one who would be honored to have such a beautiful and intelligent daughter. "She left to check on the few remaining patients about fifteen minutes ago. I'm expecting her back in around an hour."

"Good, though I can't help thinking it's going to be

a long day." The woman placed a cup along with a teaspoon on the table in front of Woody.

The man eyed them through narrowed slits. "What's going on with Katie?"

Mrs. Holden explained the situation to him quickly, ending with, "So we're just hoping to get through the next twenty-four hours without Mr. McDaniels having to run into Katie again."

Woody leaned back in his chair. "She's a sight better person than I am, letting that old coot stay here after he's treated her like that."

Josh agreed. Katie handled the situation with a kindness he wasn't sure he had. But she'd been that way even as a young girl, always trying to look at things from the other person's perspective. It was what made her a good doctor and a wonderful woman.

"Why do you look like something the cat dragged in?" Through the mist of steaming coffee, Woody studied him.

"Be nice," Mrs. Holden admonished, waving a dish towel at Josh. "Josh sat up with that man for the last two nights. Going to make himself sick if he doesn't watch it."

Woody shoveled a heaping spoonful of sugar into his mug. "Why don't I take your watch tonight?"

Josh stared into his coffee. It may only be one night, but the thought of the threats McDaniels had made turned Josh's blood cold. How would he feel if something happened to Katie, and he'd done nothing to stop it? No, it was only one more night. Tomorrow, the sheriff would accompany Mr. McDaniels to his daughter's home in Chicago. Then Josh could concentrate on his own muddled mess, including trying to figure out how to combine his new life in Kansas with his newfound love for Katie.

A motherly hand closed over his shoulder. He looked

up to find Mrs. Holden standing over him, her expression soft and understanding. "Josh, Woody here knows how to handle this kind of situation. He fought with Sam Houston."

Josh glanced at the man. "*The* Sam Houston?"

Planting his massive forearm on the table, Woody leaned in. "Is there any other?"

Josh fought to keep from chuckling. The man didn't look like any soldier he'd seen around the Citadel, but looks could be deceiving. "I'd be much obliged for your help."

A wide smile parted Woody's scraggly whiskers. "I'd do anything for Katie Bug."

"Me, too." Josh took another sip, but it could have been mud for all he knew. He'd reached the same conclusion huddled outside of McDaniels's door last night. He'd do whatever he had to for his sweet Katie. Slay her dragons, wipe away her tears. Anything to have that gentle smile of hers beaming in his direction.

But where would Katie fit into his life? He'd made a commitment to Mr. Mabry and the other farmers. Katie wouldn't leave her father and the practice she was building to follow him through Indian country. *Lord, I need some answers. Please give me wisdom to see Your will for both mine and Katie's lives.*

Mrs. Holden walked over to a small table sprinkled with flour and pulled a dishcloth from a rising lump of dough. "After we get some breakfast in you, you need to get some rest."

Josh smiled. Katie was blessed to have such a maternal soul like Mrs. Holden looking out for her. "I will, but I thought I might get Katie to show me around the college this afternoon."

A filmy white cloud of flour rose up in the air as Mrs. Holden pounded her fist into the dough. "I don't know if I would do that."

"Why?"

"It's just the professors." Woody hesitated, one side of his mouth hitching into a confused smirk. "They don't feel that a true lady should be teaching men."

"That doesn't make sense. There are female students enrolled at the college," Josh stated, exasperated. "What do they expect these ladies to do once they've completed their course work?"

Woody brought his cup to his lips and took a long sip. "Ethan has asked them that same question many times over without a satisfactory response. He tried to get Katie to quit tutoring, but she says it's not fair to the students. Truth is, I don't think she has it in her to give up."

No, Josh thought with a knowing grin. The woman had a stubborn streak a mile wide. When she set her heart to something, best to simply get out of the way of all that determination. The board of Hillsdale College didn't know what they had unleashed.

That still didn't solve his problem—keeping Katie shielded from Mr. McDaniels—but these two should have some insight between them. "What do you think Katie might enjoy doing this afternoon?"

Mrs. Holden flipped the dough over and reached for her rolling pin. "She's got a lot of friends over at the boardinghouse. Maybe you could take her over for another visit."

And risk running into Principal Whipple? Katie would never be accepted by her peers at the college. "Anything else?"

"She plays chess when she can find an opponent," Woody offered. "But that's not often."

Though he had never mastered the game, watching Katie across the board held a great deal of appeal. "She's that good?"

Woody chuckled. "That bad. I told her to stick to checkers."

Mrs. Holden lifted the rolling pin and shook it at Woody. "She's just started to learn the game. Give her some time, and she'll whip everyone under the table."

"Probably," Josh agreed, thinking it wouldn't be so bad to lose to Katie. An afternoon of chess in the front parlor might be just the diversion he was looking for.

"It's your move."

"Hmm?" Josh blinked, pushing away the cobwebs that had clouded his brain this evening, and focused on Katie. She looked so serious, studying the chessboard, her white teeth pressed into a straight line against her bottom lip. His mouth tingled at the memory of their brief kiss. What he'd give to lean over, gently trap her delicate chin between his fingers and taste the soft, supple sweetness of her lips.

"What are you thinking about so hard over there?"

"Nothing." He lowered his gaze to the board, praying that she wouldn't notice the heat climbing up his neck. "Just give me a moment."

"Are you trying to figure out your next move?"

Josh glanced up to find Katie, one cheek resting in the palm of her hand, her head tilted slightly as if giving her the perfect angle to study the board. If only she knew how close she was to the truth. That instead of sleeping this morning, he'd tossed and turned, his thoughts whirling between Katie, his commitments to the farmers and the marriage contract.

Finally, he'd gotten up and snatched his Bible out of his medical bag, flipping through the worn pages until he'd come to the verses he sought.

To every thing there is a season, and a time to every purpose under the heaven.

Was this his season to find love with Katie?

"Josh—" her voice was soft with understanding "—if you want to quit, it's all right."

"No." Josh focused on the board once more. Woody hadn't given her chess game enough credit. Logical and intelligent, her only weakness seemed to be a slight lack of confidence in her moves. All she needed was a few more victories under her belt. He made his move. "Check."

Katie glanced at him, one perfect brow arched. "Are you sure about that?"

That was his problem. He hadn't been sure about anything since Katie had come into his life again. "Yes."

Her eyes danced with amusement as she made her move. "Checkmate."

"What?" He stared down at the board, his heart thundering in his chest at the happiness radiating from her. It had been worth throwing the game just to catch a brief glimpse of her luminous smile, the sparkle that made her brown eyes shimmer with specks of gold dust. "Well done."

"I don't know if I would say that." She gave him a shy look as she reset the board. "My opponent's mind was a million miles away."

Katie shrugged deeper into the shawl she'd thrown over her shoulders. When had the large chunks of wood burned down into a few hot coals? Josh rose and headed toward the hearth. "I'm sorry. It's been an interesting last couple of days."

"That's an understatement." Her soft chuckle rippled through him like a warm ocean wave. "And it's not over yet."

"You don't have to worry about Mr. McDaniels. Charlie sent over his train ticket this morning." Grabbing the poker, Josh spread the piles of embers into a thin coat. "The sheriff is escorting him to his family in Chicago."

"It'll be good for him to be with his daughter right now. Maybe then he can start to heal."

Josh placed a large piece of seasoned oak on the fire. "If he chooses to."

"You mean, unlike our fathers?"

The flames hissed and popped as they licked their way across the aged tinder before settling deep inside the oak's rings, much like the resentment Josh felt torch through him at the thought of all the wasted moments in the past seven years.

"You want to know what I remember the most about your father?" He sensed the smile in her voice as she rose and moved around the room. "One evening, your parents threw a small dinner for just a few close friends, and as luck would have it, I was the youngest member of the party. It had already been decided that you would join the adults, which I guess was fine. You were almost fourteen. But Mama was determined that I would spend the evening in the nursery."

"I remember that," Josh replied, turning toward her, the long-ago memory settling over him like a warm blanket. "I believe there was some foot stamping on your part."

She lifted her chin slightly, as if she found the suggestion impertinent, but her wide smile and sparkling eyes confirmed his memory. "Anyway, your father came to my rescue. Not only did he charm Mama into allowing me to stay, he danced with me. My very first grown-up dance."

"Father always thought of others, especially Mother."

"It wasn't until later that I realized how truly thoughtful he'd been toward me. He had put himself in my place, and made a decision to make that evening one I still cherish."

Josh stared into the fire. Was that what Father had done for his mother? Searching for treatments because he knew that was what she wanted? "I wished I could have done something to help him with his grief."

"You did everything you could. But it's up to him whether he embraces life and decides to be happy. Those are choices we have to make for ourselves." Katie's fingers slid over his palm, threading through his until, palm to palm, their hands clasped. "But we can ask the Lord to work on his heart."

He'd never thought to pray about this problem, figured it was his cross to bear. *Or was it that I couldn't trust You, Lord? Did my pride get in the way of helping my father?* Josh squeezed her hand. "Would you pray for me, too?"

"I've always prayed for you, Josh. Even when we were apart." Katie leaned her head against his shoulder. "That's what friends do."

In that moment, resting his cheek against Katie's silky hair, Josh knew. He'd never see the Kansas Territory, never practice medicine out West, not unless Katie stood by his side, his mother's wedding ring on her left hand.

But she didn't want to marry him. She'd said as much when he'd told her about the marriage contract. Of course she'd say that! What woman wouldn't when he'd almost accused her of buying a husband?

What do I do here, Lord?

A plan formed almost instantly in Josh's head. He'd court her, prove that his feelings for her had changed from friendship to lifelong love.

But first, he needed to speak with Dr. Clark and get this marriage contract settled. Tonight.

"Dr. Clark?" Josh knocked on the open door. Katie's father had taken to spending his evenings in his office, his leg propped up on a velvet-lined ottoman while he perused the pile of charts and papers that tilted at a slight angle on his desk. The faint sweet scent of pipe tobacco hung in the air. It was a man's sanctuary, if ever there was one.

"Come in."

Josh stepped inside, looking toward the area behind the desk where he expected Dr. Clark to be, but it was empty. A slight movement to his left caught his eye, and he turned. The older man leaned heavily upon one of the many bookcases in the room while Mrs. Holden stood with her back to him, a rosy red coloring her neck all the way to the tips of her ears.

It seemed Josh wasn't the only one interested in courting. "I'm sorry. I can come back later."

"I need to get back to the kitchen if I want to have everything ready for breakfast in the morning," Mrs. Holden answered in a breathless rush, her face still flushed with color.

"Good night, Marianne," Clark said, the words low and tender, almost like a soft caress.

"Ethan," the older woman answered with a delicate smile, her eyes shining with happiness and something akin to hope. She hurried across the room to the door before seeming to remember something, and she turned toward them. "Good night, Dr. McClain."

Neither man spoke until the door clicked shut. "I'm sorry, Dr. Clark. I thought you were alone."

"I'm never alone." The man hobbled around his desk to his chair, then carefully lowered himself into it, motioning Josh to sit down. "But then, a man can have the entire world around him and still be lonely, all because he thinks he's doing the right thing. Life catches up with you, and what you thought was for the best isn't so cut-and-dried anymore."

"You mean Mrs. Holden."

Clark nodded as he lifted his wounded leg onto the ottoman. "I should have married her long ago, but I wasn't sure how Katie would handle the situation."

"Maybe you should have asked Katie."

Chuckling, he leaned back in his chair. "Knowing Katie, she probably would have surprised me."

Josh nodded. Yes, Katie had certainly surprised him. "She's why I need to talk to you."

The older man leaned back in his chair, his fingers steepled over his chest. "You want to know about the marriage contract."

"Well, yes." All Josh's questions flew out of his head except for one. "Why did you and my father enter into such an agreement in the first place?"

A faint smile lifted the corners of the older man's mouth. "Your father thought it was a ridiculous idea, but your mother…she had her mind made up and nothing was going to change it."

A fever of hot and cold sensations flushed through Josh. "Mother was behind this?"

"She sent a note to me a couple of days before Katie and I were supposed to leave Charleston. I knew that Reba didn't have long, and I think she knew that, too, because she was using what was left of her energy to get her life in order."

He remembered those days, a fury of doctors in and out of the house, his father with a wide-eyed frenzied look that only grew more hopeless with every passing second. That his mother had remained so calm was a testament to her faith in Christ. "Why did she want the contract?"

"Reba thought I was running away, coming to Hillsdale so soon after Millicent died." He snorted softly. "Maybe she was just a little bit right, but that's in the past. Her biggest concerns were you and Katie."

"Sounds like Mother. She loved Katie as if she was her own."

"Which is why she called me to your house that day. She felt that with our move to Michigan, you and Katie would lose touch just when you needed each other the most."

Mother had been right about that, too. He'd needed Katie, yearned for her company in those difficult months after his mother's passing. "I thought Katie had forgotten about me until you told me about the letters. I just wish I had received them."

Clark shook his head. "I've been thinking about that and it seems to me you might want to ask Samuel if he kept them. I can't see him throwing something that precious away."

"I doubt Father bothered himself with something like that."

"Give Samuel a bit more credit than that. He was hurting badly, and the last thing he'd want for you is to feel the kind of pain he himself was going through."

There was some truth to what Clark said, Josh acknowledged grudgingly, though the Samuel McClain the older man knew no longer existed. How might Josh have looked at his life if he'd known about Katie's letters, known that she'd still cared about him?

"Why did you come here, Josh?"

A week ago, he'd been certain his only reason for coming was to break the marriage agreement, but now he wondered if it hadn't been curiosity, as well. To see Katie again, find out what kind of woman she'd become, maybe… Josh blinked. Maybe to discover if the feelings he had begun to feel for Katie back then were real or just a passing fancy. "Mother knew I would come here, didn't she? She knew I wouldn't move ahead with my life without getting this contract settled."

"She counted on that responsible streak in you, and it's served her well." Clark smiled.

"Is the contract even valid?"

"No, it never was. The only reason I can think your father would show it to you is that he promised Reba he would."

"And the money?"

"A loan your father paid back many years ago." The older man studied Josh as if he were a specimen under a magnifying glass. "So, tell me, son, what are you doing here?"

There were still some things he needed to work out with his father, but the answers Dr. Clark had given him loosened the vise that had gripped his heart, giving him hope for the future.

A future with Katie.

Straightening in his chair, Josh met Dr. Clark's piercing gaze. "I'm going to be honest with you, sir. If she'll have me, I want to marry Katie."

"I hear a *but* in there."

"Well, the thing is I can't open a practice—at least not one here in Hillsdale. I won't do that to Katie."

Clark leaned back in his chair, crossing his arms over his waist. "What if I retire?"

"Does Katie know about this?"

He chuckled. "Oh, I've told her several times, but she's never taken me very seriously—not that she's had a reason to." The older man sobered. "Truth is, my heart's just not in treating patients anymore, but I feared that the town council wouldn't accept Katie taking over our practice."

"Have you talked to them about this?"

Clark nodded. "Several times, and it's always been the same. They won't hire her on unless she has a partner."

The thought appealed to Josh, sharing a practice and a home with Katie. But how would she feel about this? Betrayed that Josh had come in and taken over what she'd worked so hard to accomplish? Or as a beginning for both of them—as both partners and man and wife?

"Hello, Dr. Katie! You look mighty pretty this morning."

Holding her medical bag in front of her, Katie stopped and smiled at the snip of a girl bouncing down the sidewalk toward her, her blond braid swinging from side to side, her right arm hanging precariously in a sling. "Why, thank you, Ginger. You're looking mighty fine this morning, too. How is your shoulder feeling?"

"Better." The child removed her arm from the thick

band of cotton, flapping it up and down like a baby bird trying to leave the nest. "I can move it real good, see?"

Lord, help this child! Katie gave the girl what she hoped was a stern look. "You should still be careful, at least for a few more days."

"Yes, ma'am." Ginger glanced up and down the sidewalk as if searching for something. "Where's Dr. McClain?"

The question surprised Katie. "Down at the train station. Why?"

"Just wanted to know." The girl flashed her a toothy smile. "Is that where you're headed? The train station, I mean?"

"No," Katie bit out. Though she didn't have a reason for being on the road that led straight to the depot, somehow she'd found herself here waiting, glancing toward the station entrance, hoping to catch a glimpse of Josh. It was silly, really. Just because he'd left with Mr. McDaniels before she'd made it downstairs this morning didn't give her a reason to feel this vague sense of disappointment. She finally admitted to herself she enjoyed seeing him at the foot of the stairs each morning, waiting to walk her into the dining room for breakfast. Josh made her feel special by the care he showed her, pouring her coffee or asking about her cases for the day. He'd fit so quickly into her life, her heart, it was as if the last puzzle piece to her happiness had slipped quietly into place.

But what about Josh, Lord? He hadn't said as much, but Katie sensed something different in the way he looked at her, an awareness she didn't quite understand. Not physical attraction, though there was plenty of that. No, this was something much more exciting, more precious than any words could describe.

"Are you betrothed to Dr. McClain?"

The question snapped Katie out of her musings. "Why would you ask something like that?"

"My aunt says you're betrothed to each other," Ginger replied, cocking her head to one side. "But I'm not sure what *betrothed* means."

"Maybe you need to keep that pretty little nose in the books more and find out." The familiar masculine voice answered just over Katie's right shoulder, close enough his breath tickled the tiny hairs on the back of her neck.

"Dr. McClain! I've been looking for you." The young girl flung herself against Josh's side, her arms wrapped tightly around Josh's waist. She buried her face in the black wool of his overcoat and took a deep breath. "Peppermint."

It seemed she wasn't the only one who knew Josh kept a stash of the candy sticks in his coat pocket. He glanced over at Katie and winked, causing her heart to flutter against her ribs like a tiny bird trapped in a cage. He'd make a good father, she thought, expecting a lot from his children, of course, but those expectations tempered by unconditional love and respect.

Josh trapped Ginger's chin between his gloved fingers and tilted her head back, a smile trying to tease its way through the stern look on his face. "Didn't I just give you a peppermint stick yesterday?"

The girl's eyes grew round. "Yes, but I gave half of it to Cynthia yesterday. She didn't have much in her lunch pail, and I thought it might make her feel better."

"That was kind of you." He tweaked her nose, then glanced over at Katie. "So what do you think? Should I give her another peppermint?"

"I don't know," she answered, glancing anywhere

but at Ginger's beseeching face. She tapped one finger against her lips. "She does need to apply herself to her studies."

"I will! I promise!"

"And we need to take into consideration she shared her first stick with a friend," Josh added, his blue eyes sparkling with playful mischief.

Katie smiled back at him. "Then I think you have no choice but to give her another one."

"Oh, thank you!" Ginger stepped back, almost prancing from side to side as Josh unbuttoned his coat and withdrew a small bag. The stiff paper softly crinkled as he crouched down and held out the open bag to the child. Ginger mashed her lips together, then asked, "Can I have one to take to Cynthia, too?"

"May I…?" Josh started.

"May I have one to take to Cynthia?"

Josh nodded. "Yes."

Ginger gave Josh a swift kiss on the cheek, then turned to the important business of picking out the perfect sticks of candy. Josh glanced at Katie, and for the first time in forever, she wondered what it would be like to have children of her own. At least two, maybe even three, with blond hair and blue eyes as soft as a South Carolina sky.

"Would you like a peppermint, Dr. Katie?"

Josh held out the paper bag to her, studying her with such intensity, she felt herself go warm. "No, but thank you anyway."

Josh stood, folding the ends of the bag up and stuffing it back into his pocket. "Boy, Cynthia must be a good friend for you to be saving her a peppermint until school tomorrow."

"I'm not saving it for school," Ginger replied, carefully

placing the two sticks in her coat pocket. "A bunch of us are sledding this afternoon at the old Tompkins place."

Katie's pulse thundered through her veins, her hands suddenly clammy inside her leather gloves. She'd visited the sledding hill right outside of town her first winter in Hillsdale, had made her first run through the snow when she'd heard a guttural yell in the small valley beside her followed by screams for the doctor. Katie had wasted no time, running toward her house as fast as her legs would carry her. The look in her father's eyes as he'd leaned over that child, the fear that had caused his hands to shake, had stayed with her. She'd seen that look only one other time.

The day her mother had died.

"I thought y'all went sledding yesterday afternoon," Josh said.

"You knew?" Katie's head jerked toward him, her teeth set.

"Ginger told me about it yesterday." He smiled at the little girl. "Thought it might be something fun to do after the last few days."

Katie drew in a shaky breath. Of course he couldn't know the dangers, she reminded herself, forcing herself to relax her jaw. Abbeville rarely got any snow, and when it did, it wasn't enough to consider sledding. "I don't know if sledding is such a good idea, Ginger."

"Why not?" the child whined.

"I think Dr. Katie worries that someone might get hurt." Josh's gaze met hers. "Isn't that right?"

How could he be so calm when her insides jittered like butter on a hot pan? "That's right, Ginger. Doctors hate to think that the people they take care of might get hurt."

"We'll be careful, I promise."

A promise she couldn't keep, not if she went sledding. "Ginger…"

"Everyone from school's going to be there, even some of the kids from the college." Ginger's mouth twisted into a determined line. "And there's a race with a prize of a dollar for the first-place sled."

Katie clutched her medical bag in both hands. Prize money! That would only serve to make people more reckless and irresponsible. Didn't the person who'd come up with this brilliant idea understand that a life could so easily be lost with that kind of reckless behavior? "What time does it start?"

Ginger stole a glance at Josh. "I'm on my way over there right now."

"Then we'd better get moving." Katie started down the sidewalk, balancing her medical bag in her hand as she tried to lift her skirt.

"Here." Josh took the leather bag from her and offered her his free arm. "Can't have you falling down and breaking your arm before we even get there."

Katie wanted to make a face at him, just as she had in the old days, but the feel of hard muscle beneath her gloved fingertips muddled every thought in her head. Instead, she nodded, letting him take the lead.

Chapter 11

He heard the delighted screams and shouts before the snow-covered hill came into view with the first sleds blading out a rough path down the slippery slope. Stocking-capped ladies pink from the cold and men in long coats and beaver-skin hats teetered at the top of the low-rising hill, cheering each sled as it hung off the edge before careening down to the small valley below.

"I'll be careful, I promise," Ginger called out over her shoulder as she scurried up the embankment, slipping and sliding, digging her mittened hands into the packed snow.

Katie's fingers tightened against his arm as another band of sledders came flying down close by. She'd been wound tighter than his watch spring ever since Ginger had mentioned this outing. After the past few days, maybe all she needed was a little reassurance. He leaned toward her, a mixture of fresh air, evergreens and lavender almost causing him to lose his train of thought. "It's not really much of a hill."

"It's enough."

"The oak you used to climb down to escape your old bedroom stands higher than this mound of dirt."

She glanced up at him, her mouth a straight tense line, her eyes troubled. "I just don't want anyone to get hurt."

A peal of laughter followed another sled down the hill, ending in a glorious scream when the riders were deposited in a bank of knee-deep snow. "Looks like everyone is having a good time."

She turned her attention back to the hill. "Next thing you know, you'll be trying to talk me into flinging myself down the side of a mountain holding on to nothing more than a rotted-out board and two rusty blades."

"You've got to admit, it does look like fun."

"It was," she whispered. "Once."

Katie couldn't have surprised him more if she'd tried. "Let me get this straight. Dr. Kathleen Clark, the same woman who almost had a fit when Ginger mentioned sledding in the first place, has actually gone sledding herself."

"The first year I moved to Hillsdale."

That girl, Josh knew very well. She'd been all of eighteen then, eager to experience life, ready to face down anyone who hurt one of God's creatures. This little hill would have been nothing to that Katie.

"Something happened."

"How do you know that?"

"I know you." Josh took her arm, his gaze falling on an old wooden bench they'd passed on their way to the hill. "Here, let's sit down and talk."

Katie glanced back toward the hill. "What if something…?"

"We can watch them from here. If anyone needs our help, we'll be close by."

With a reluctant nod, Katie slid her hand into his. The narrow path leading to the bench had been cleared as had the bench, giving onlookers a comfortable place to view the sledding. Josh reached into his pocket and retrieved the clean handkerchief Mrs. Holden had given him that morning, unfolding and draping it across the wooden slats of the seat.

"My lady." He bent slightly at the waist.

Katie sank down on the bench, then glanced back up at him. "You probably think I'm a ninny or something."

He sat down beside her, taking her gloved hand between his, noting how delicate and small it felt. "I'd just like to know what happened."

She pressed her lips together, almost as if she was struggling for the words. "The first time I came here, one of the younger boys from school was thrown clear of his sled and hit a tree." She glanced up to the summit. "Everyone came over that hill like ants scurrying around aimlessly, not sure if Abe was alive or dead."

"What did you do?"

"I ran as hard as I could to get Papa."

"You always did think fast on your feet." Josh squeezed her hand gently between his. "So, what happened?"

"Abe was unconscious for a little while, but eventually he recovered."

Not the ending of the story he'd expected. "I'm confused."

The delicate muscles in her throat rippled as she swallowed hard. "When Papa knelt down to examine Abe, there was this look he gave me, this frantic, fearful look as if he was imagining it was Mama lying there, and he was helpless to do anything."

Josh understood Dr. Clark's feelings. His father had behaved the same way when his mother slowly faded away in the weeks after the accident. "It's normal to feel like that."

"I know." Her back rigid, she turned, her knee brushing up against his. "But that night, he railed at me. How could I do something so dangerous? Didn't I know what could happen if something went wrong?" Her gaze fell to her fisted hand in her lap. "I just couldn't bear being a disappointment to him, too."

As I was to my mother. Josh didn't have to hear the words—he could read them in the pinched expression around her eyes and the way she tightened and flexed her fingers in the folds of her skirt. It was a wonder Katie had made it through medical school, what with the memory of her mother's disapproval taunting her at every turn.

But Dr. Clark's motives may have been different. Lifting one hand from hers, he cupped the fragile line of her jaw and tilted her head back. A fringe of golden-brown lashes glistened in the pale sunlight, and Josh struggled with the urge to kiss those unshed tears away. "I think you misunderstood your father."

Katie's eyes flew open. "He said he was disappointed in me."

"A lot of times people say the wrong thing when they're terrified of losing someone they love."

"Why would he…?"

Josh smiled at her confusion. "He'd just lost your mother, Katie, and here he was presented with a severely injured child who was sledding like you were. Of course his mind jumped to the possibility of losing you. He probably couldn't bear the thought." Josh knew he couldn't.

She pondered this for a moment. "Then why didn't he just say so?"

"People don't react very logically when deep emotions are involved." He traced his thumb across the apple of her cheek, enjoying the splash of color blooming under his fingertips.

"That would explain why it's so hard to tell someone you love them."

His heart jumped when she pressed her cheek deeper into the palm of his hand. She was a beauty, lovelier than anything he ever deserved. He leaned toward her, resting his forehead against hers, drowning in the deep warm depths of her dark brown eyes. A question fluttered through his mind and was on his lips before he could stop it. "Are you in love, Katie Bug?"

Her mouth parted in surprise. It probably wasn't fair, but he seized the moment. Winding his hand around to the back of her neck, he brushed his mouth against hers. The tiny sigh she released against his lips sent a wave of pure male pride humming through him, and he deepened the kiss.

"Is this what *betrothed* means?" a girlish voice asked.

They jumped apart, Katie rising to her feet. How the woman stood, Josh didn't know, though she did seem to wobble just a bit. Or was that just wishful thinking on his part? He leaned back against the bench. "Ginger, is something wrong?"

The child's gaze bounced between the two of them, her smile a tad too impish for comfort. "No, just the race is about to begin. Don't you and Dr. Katie want to watch?"

"We were in the middle..." Josh started.

"Yes, yes, we would," Katie finished, flashing him an annoyed look. "We'll be right there."

"I'll tell everyone to wait on you." Ginger turned, hop-scotching through the snow toward the crowd gathered at the bottom of the sledding hill.

Katie whirled around to face him. "You know Ginger is going to tell everyone who will listen that she caught us…"

"Kissing, Katie. We shared a kiss. Men and women do that occasionally."

The guilty expression in her eyes softened a bit, and her lips twitched into a slight smile. "I know that, but everyone in town is going to think that…"

"We're getting married? Maybe we should. We already finish each other's sentences like an old married couple," he answered, grabbing his handkerchief off the bench and stuffing it into his pocket.

"I don't think reading each other's thoughts is a good basis for a lifelong commitment, do you?"

"No," he answered, pushing himself up from the bench. But did Katie realize what they did have? Respect for each other, shared interests, a faith in God. Love. "You never answered my question."

Color flushed her cheeks again. "I can't answer it yet, Josh."

His heart refused to beat. "Why?"

She lifted her chin, her gaze meeting and catching his. "Have you heard anything from the gentleman in Kansas yet?"

Josh's heart leaped in his chest. When he did put a ring on her finger, it would be a gold band that held a sparkle like her eyes. "Mabry has promised to let me know by Thursday."

She gave a little nod, then turned to go.

"Katie?"

She stopped, calling back over her shoulder. "Yes?"

"May I escort you to the St. Valentine's social at the college Thursday afternoon?"

Katie hesitated, and he wondered: Was it possible that she didn't feel the same way he did? Or could she just be protecting her heart? Whatever reservations she might have had, she evidently pushed them aside because she turned to him and smiled. "It begins at four o'clock."

"You look like perfection!"

Katie looked into the full-length mirror as Liberty lifted the small train of her new dress and let it float slowly down over her petticoats. She'd been a bit skeptical when her friend had suggested a mint-green silk instead of a more workable blue or black, but the pale confection Liberty had designed made Katie feel uniquely feminine, beautiful for the first time in her life. Or was it Josh who made her feel that way?

Liberty came up alongside her, picking at Katie's sleeves until they met her approval. "Your Dr. McClain won't be able to take his eyes off of you."

"He's not my Dr. McClain." Not yet anyway. But Katie hadn't missed the telegram that had been delivered to the house late that afternoon, nor the fact that Josh had gone straight to her father's study immediately after getting it. What it contained, she still didn't know, only that Mr. Mabry's answer had the power to break her heart.

Liberty's eyes met hers in the mirror. "That's not what I've heard."

Katie's mouth went dry. "Has Ginger been busy telling tales?"

"Ginger? Isn't that Principal Whipple's niece?" Liberty's mouth blossomed into a wide smile. "What kinds of tales could that girl have on you, Miss Prim-and-Proper-Dr. Katie?"

Oh, dear! Heat swept across her chest and up her neck as she thought of the feel of Josh's lips caressing hers, his hand at the nape of her neck. "Is it a little warm in here?"

Liberty's jaw dropped open, and then as if remembering her upbringing, she closed her mouth. "He kissed you at the sledding hill! Why didn't I see that?"

"Maybe you were too busy hanging on to the handsome young man you asked me to examine the other day."

It was Liberty's turn to blush. "You're right. It is hot in here." She walked over to the window and cracked it open. The cool air felt wonderfully comfortable against Katie's skin.

Liberty leaned with her back against the wall. "That gentleman you saw me with was Gerrett. Gerrett Divine. He's one of my brother's oldest friends."

Gathering up her skirts, Katie walked over to where Liberty stood, then leaned back against the wall beside her. "Is this the man who burst into the kitchen the day after the wreck and asked you to forgive him?"

"Ursula told you, huh?"

Katie nodded. "So, tell me about him."

"There's not much to tell." Sadness dulled Liberty's voice as if this wasn't the fairy-tale ending she'd always hoped for herself. "He's engaged to be married."

"Have you been in love with him a long time?"

She gave a slight nod. "I've had feelings for him most of my life. What about you and Dr. McClain?"

Katie's heart banged uncomfortably against her ribs. "What about us?"

"Woody's been telling everyone all over town that the two of you are betrothed."

"I guess, in a sense we are."

Liberty turned, leaning one shoulder against the wall. "I don't understand."

"I fell in love with Josh when I was fourteen." Katie hesitated, then told her friend the whole story of their mothers' deaths in a carriage accident, of waiting patiently for some answer to the weekly letters she'd written him, of the heartache when month after month there had been no reply, of finding him in the wreckage of the train accident, of the marriage contract their fathers had drawn up. "So, there you have it. It's a mess, isn't it?"

"Does Josh still want to break the marriage contract?"

"I don't know." Katie sighed, slumping against the wall. "I've been too afraid to ask him. But whether he does or doesn't, I don't want him to marry me out of some sense of obligation." Her voice cracked. "Commitments and obligations are very important to him."

"Oh, Katie." Liberty gave her a worried look. "Why did you agree to go with him to the social today?"

"Because I couldn't say no." Katie pushed away from the wall and strolled over to the mirrors, straightening her back to accentuate the delicate lines of Liberty's creation. If she was correct and Mr. Mabry's telegram arrived today, Josh could be on the first train out in the morning, and all she would be left with were memories of their few brief days together.

Liberty tugged at the handkerchief she kept hidden at her wrist and touched it to her nose as she walked back to Katie. "There's just one thing I don't understand."

"What's that?"

"Why did he tell me this morning that he was your fiancé?"

Wouldn't it be lovely if Josh was truly hers? Katie shrugged. "Probably didn't want to embarrass me further."

"Maybe he's changed his mind."

Oh, how Katie wished that was so. "Josh only thinks of me as his childhood friend."

The comical look Liberty gave her almost made Katie smile. "Even I know enough to understand men don't go around kissing their childhood friends."

Katie nodded in agreement. But did that mean Josh had feelings for her, that he might want to marry her?

"Have you prayed about it?"

"Yes," Katie answered automatically, but the word caught in her throat. Oh, she'd asked God to send Josh packing, and then as their friendship rekindled, that He would allow Josh to stay. But had she simply lifted up her love for Josh and asked God to reveal His heart on the matter? Would she have heard Him if He did? Shame washed over her. "No, Liberty. I haven't prayed about this like I should have. I'm afraid to."

Liberty put her arm around Katie's waist and pulled her close. "Because you're afraid God will say no?"

"Or yes." The words felt thick against her tongue. "And then Josh would end up resenting me for being another obligation he had to meet. Why can't things just stay the way they are?"

"What fun would that be? Besides, aren't you the one always reminding me that God has a time for every purpose? That everything has a season?" Liberty smiled at her in the glass. "Maybe this is your time to find love with Josh?"

"And if it isn't?"

"Then God has a better plan for you, and for Josh."

Katie knew that, had clung to that knowledge so many times in the past. But it still didn't stop the feeling of loss that slid through her. Why would God allow Josh back into her life only to take him away again?

Not my will, but Thine, Lord.

"Will you pray with me, Liberty?" Katie held out her hand to her friend.

Liberty grasped her hand and held it tight. "If you'll pray for me, too."

"Always." Then Katie bowed her head, and all other thoughts faded as she went before her Father in prayer.

Chapter 12

"We heard you're from South Carolina, Dr. McClain."

Josh glanced over the rim of his coffee cup at the bevy of young ladies surrounding him, their eyelashes fluttering in time with their fans. He'd thought young women attending college would be prone to more serious subjects such as literature or the sciences, not the art of flirtation.

His hypothesis had been proved wrong.

The Valentine's social was in full swing, and still no Katie. His gaze wandered around the large room, the crowd clumped together in smaller groups of four or five. Josh had almost balked when Katie had suggested they make their rounds—he wanted her all to himself this afternoon. To talk about the telegram he'd received from Mr. Mabry. About the discussions her father had had with the town council regarding his retirement. To chart out the rest of their lives.

"Hillsdale must be quite different from your home."

"Yes, I imagine it is," he answered. Ah, there Katie was, talking with that Whipple woman and two rather distinguished-looking gentlemen he had yet to meet. She looked particularly lovely today, the mint-green confection her friend had designed complementing her creamy complexion, giving her a glow he found completely irresistible. She tilted her head slightly, a habit he'd noticed whenever her mind drifted.

Not that he could blame her. Over the past two days, Josh had found his own thoughts bouncing in every direction, all centering back on Katie.

"But you can't possibly like the weather after living in Charleston," a young woman who'd been introduced as Miss Adams said. "I detest the cold."

"It's not so bad," Josh responded. Especially if it meant sitting by the fireplace, playing chess with Katie, going over the events of their day together.

Two more men, students from what Josh could tell, joined Katie's group, one standing on either side of her. Of course she'd draw them to her, like honeybees to the perfect bloom.

It was time to claim his lady. Josh placed his cup on a nearby tray. "If you'll excuse me, I need to check on Dr. Clark."

"Oh, yes. Mr. Woods mentioned something about a betrothal," a blonde to his left said behind her fan. "We weren't quite sure what to make of it."

Irritation straightened Josh to his full height. "What do you mean?"

"Well, it's just that…it seemed understood that Dr. Clark would never marry, not with the profession she's chosen."

Lord, please guard my tongue. Help me with my temper. "Miss Marks, is it?"

She nodded.

"Do you feel that all physicians should remain unmarried because of their profession? Because that's what you're implying."

Her gray eyes grew round over the top of her fan. "Why, no, but..."

"But what? All physicians should not marry by reason of their profession. That's your hypothesis."

A young woman to his right leaned heavily on her friend. "My papa's a doctor. I couldn't imagine him without Mama."

"And what about my Benard? He's studying medicine."

"You misunderstand, Dr. McClain," Miss Marks replied.

"Then please explain yourself," he said with a calmness he didn't think possible.

All attention turned to Miss Marks, who had blushed herself into a vivid shade of bright red. Her gaze shifted from one person to the next, looking to be rescued, then with a sharp flutter of her fan, she excused herself.

"Please, excuse Edith, Dr. McClain. She's always had it in for Katie," one young lady murmured. "It's because her father's a doctor. He doesn't think there's a place for women in the medical field."

Miss Langley gave him a look of admiration. "Katie is very blessed to have you to defend her."

"Thank you, but if anyone is blessed, it is myself for knowing her," he murmured, giving them a slight bow as he excused himself.

The hall suddenly seemed overflowing. Children of

all ages and sizes hopped around the small musical ensemble. Gray light filtered in through a line of windows, supplemented by dozens of candles in silver candelabras. The scent of spices and apple cider weighed heavily in the air. Josh glanced toward Miss Whipple and her group, but Katie wasn't anywhere to be found.

"Dr. McClain. Just the man I was looking for."

Josh scowled. Not much of a Valentine's Day social if he couldn't spend time with the woman who held his heart. He closed his eyes for a brief moment and breathed, then turned his attention to a tall, portly man hurrying toward him. "Dr. Etheridge, how are you this afternoon?"

"Good." Pride filled the man's expression as he glanced over the room. "The social is going very well, very well indeed. I think our unexpected guests will leave Hillsdale with a vastly different perception of our little town."

Josh nodded. Hillsdale had only been another stop along the way to his new life in Kansas when he'd boarded the train in Chicago. Now this place would become his home, a home he hoped to build with Katie.

"I talked with Dr. Clark this morning. We've finally reached an agreement concerning his practice. Now all we need to do is settle the financial arrangements with you and Miss Clark."

"Dr. Clark," Josh corrected. "And it is understood that I will be a junior partner."

"Yes, yes," the man blustered. "Of course, Ethan will continue teaching at the college. But it will be a huge blow to the community."

Yes, Josh conceded. For a town accustomed to having two physicians for the price of one, it was a loss. "Then

Hillsdale is blessed to have Katie ready to take over her father's practice."

"I agree."

Josh studied the man. "You do?"

At least Etheridge had the decency to look ashamed. "I'll admit I've not given Katie fair consideration as a doctor. But she changed my mind, and the minds of the council members, by her professionalism after the train accident—particularly the way she conducted herself with Mr. McDaniels."

Josh smiled. Oh, how he wished Katie could hear these accolades herself! She'd worked so hard to get the folks in Hillsdale to trust her as a doctor, and now it seemed her prayers had been answered. "You ought to let Katie know that, Dr. Etheridge."

"Yes, well..." Etheridge cleared his throat. "I'm just glad you're staying on here in Hillsdale. There will always be those reluctant to change their ways or their minds about certain things." The man held up his hand when Josh would have spoken. "Despite people's unwillingness to embrace the future, it's this town's obligation to supply its citizens with someone to care for them."

Etheridge had a point. The last thing Josh wanted was for Katie to go somewhere she wasn't respected. "Dr. Clark and I will do our best to provide good medical care to everyone."

The man brightened noticeably. "Good, good. Hillsdale has grown used to having two fine doctors for our community, and we're growing larger every day. Why, several of the passengers in the train wreck have decided to make our little town their new home." He clapped Josh on the shoulder. "Including you."

"Yes, well, there are still some things that need to be

settled before I can sign the contracts," Josh answered, looking for a means of escape. He needed to find Katie and get those very things settled. Because he couldn't consider any position and couldn't think of staying in Hillsdale if he had no chance of winning her heart.

"Well, you'd better get things settled because the town council is extremely happy with the arrangements we've made to bring you on as a town doctor."

A gasp seemed to echo in the air around Josh, and he turned, his heart dropping to the pit of his stomach when he saw her. Katie stared at him, her cheeks drained of color, the pale shade of her gown suddenly too garish against her skin. "Congratulations, Josh," she whispered.

"Katie?" He stepped toward her.

But she didn't answer, didn't even look up at him as she gathered the swells of her skirts in her clenched hands and ran toward the exit.

Josh hurried after Katie, but the woman was quick, sliding in and out of the crowd like a doe pursued by a hunter. A patch of green floated into view and he turned, barely avoiding a collision with an older gentleman leaning heavily on a wooden cane.

"Pardon me, sir," he said apologetically over his shoulder, paying no mind to the scowl that creased the man's face. All that mattered to him right now was heading toward the nearest door. If he could just have a moment with her, relay the conversation with Dr. Etheridge in its entirety, Katie would see reason. She had to.

Their future depended on it.

He couldn't see her now, the tide of people filling the hall to its very seams. Where could she have disappeared off to so quickly?

"Dr. McClain?"

"Yes," he snapped, jerking around to where Miss Langley stood, her hands calmly folded over her waist.

"Katie took the side door out." She nodded to a paneled door along a near wall. "Over there."

"Where does it go?"

She smiled softly. "To the chapel."

"Bless you, Miss Langley."

Josh barely noticed the girl's blush as he turned and headed in that direction.

The cold air stole across his exposed skin, a refreshing change after the crush in the great hall. A few people, mainly couples wishing to spend a few moments alone with their valentines, lined the walls, their faces hidden in the gray shadows along the breezeway. Josh spied a door to his left and hurried toward it.

Low-hanging clouds had begun spitting out bits and pieces of ice and snow again, stinging Josh's face and hands like tiny needles. The chapel sat off in the distance, the freshly fallen snow making it look like one of the pastoral paintings Josh's mother had loved so much. He started down the pathway, then paused.

Instead of one set of boot prints, there were two.

Katie pressed her back against the closed chapel door and shut her eyes. She'd worked so hard, taken every slight that had been thrown at her, doctored into the night without any hope of being paid for her services, of being respected for her abilities. And for what? So that the town council could offer her job to someone else? Granted, that man was Josh, but how could they do this to her after all she'd done to prove herself?

How could Josh even consider accepting the position?

Why does no one choose me, Lord? What do I have to do to prove myself worthy?

Bible verses floated along the fringes of her memory before taking center stage. *Blessed be the God and Father of our Lord Jesus Christ, who hath blessed us with all spiritual blessings in heavenly places in Christ according as He hath chosen us in Him before the foundation of the world, that we should be holy and without blame before Him in love: having predestinated us unto the adoption of children by Jesus Christ to Himself, according to the good pleasure of His will.*

The words rained over her, soaking into her parched soul. She had been chosen, before the earth and the stars came into existence. A child of God by grace. Katie drew in a deep breath, a peace she'd always felt just out of her reach settling over her like a warm quilt. The Lord of heaven and earth had chosen her despite her foolish self.

It was more than she had ever hoped for. "Thank You, Lord."

A gust of cold wind blew in through the cracks in the door, causing her to shiver. She couldn't go back to the party, not yet anyway. But standing in the freezing alcove wasn't an option either.

The sanctuary was warmer, but not by much. Katie walked farther up the aisle before settling into the seat she usually occupied with Liberty for Sunday services. That was when she noticed him. A man, a few rows in front of her.

She couldn't place him, though something about the way he held himself hinted of familiarity. But did it matter? He'd probably come here to pray and look for solace just as she had. She only prayed he found it.

Several moments passed as Katie contemplated her

life. She couldn't stay in Hillsdale and practice medicine. That much was apparent. Maybe she'd go west, find a town willing to take on a woman doctor.

What about Papa? His plan had always been to continue teaching at the college. Would he be disappointed in her if she left Hillsdale? Or would he understand?

To every thing, there is a season.

And Josh? He'd be a wonderful town doctor, with his friendly manner and that silly bag of peppermint sticks he always carried around in his pocket. Of all the people on this earth, he understood her the most, made her feel like a partner in the truest sense of the word.

A time to love.

A shadow fell across her, taking with it the last rays of the sun's warmth. She glanced up, her heart lunging into her throat as she pressed herself farther into the pew. This wasn't possible. He was supposed to be in Chicago.

"Hello, Dr. Clark."

Out of the corner of her eye, she saw something glimmering at the man's waist. A gun? Her stomach turned in a sickening twist.

Dear Lord, I need You! Help me!

"Good afternoon, Mr. McDaniels."

"May I sit down?"

Katie nodded, though just barely. Josh had put this man on the westbound train just two days ago. How had McDaniels made it back to Hillsdale so quickly and without anyone noticing him? "I thought you'd gone to your daughter's home in Chicago."

McDaniels sank down beside her, clasping his hands in a tight knot in his lap. "I did. Saw my new grandson. Molly's grandson. He's beautiful."

Katie nodded. "Babies usually are."

"He looks just like her, you know. Got his grandma's big blue eyes. And he's always got them wide open, staring at everything as if he's taking it all in."

"Molly would have been so proud."

He nodded, his mouth lifting in a sad smile. "He got me thinking, my grandson, that is. About those verses in Lamentations, the ones about a time to be born and a time to die."

Ecclesiastes, but she wasn't about to correct him, not when she wasn't sure whose death he was referring to yet. "I know the ones."

"Little Adam, that's what they call him, after my papa. Well, it's Adam's time to be born, to walk this earth, to make his mark on the world," he said, lowering his head. "Just like it was Molly's time to die."

Katie blew out a shaky breath. "I know."

Lifting his head, he turned to look at her, his blue eyes dulled to a mournful gray. "I should not have blamed you for what happened to Molly, not when you were just trying to help her."

"You were hurting, Mr. McDaniels. I knew that."

The man held up one hand. "Still, I took out all my anger about the train wreck, about what happened to Molly, on you, then you let me stay in your home. That wasn't right of me, acting like that. My wife never would have stood for that kind of behavior."

Katie placed her hand on his forearm. "I forgive you, Mr. McDaniels, though I believe there's nothing to forgive."

"Thank you." He sniffed, then, placing his hands on the pew in front of him, pulled himself to his feet. "Well, I'm heading back to my daughter's in the morning, so if I don't see you again—" he seemed to stumble on the words "—thank you for helping my Molly."

"Have a safe journey home."

McDaniels stepped out into the aisle, then with a nod, strode slowly toward the vestibule. Katie dropped her face in her hands, her body shivering at the riot of emotions running through her. *Thank You, Lord. Thank You for keeping me safe. I was so scared but You were with me.*

A pair of warm arms circled her shoulders, drawing her into the comfort of a muscular male chest. Her senses registered the faint scent of fresh air and peppermint she always connected with Josh, and she sagged against him. "He came to apologize to me."

"I heard," he whispered against her hair, his arms tightening around her. "I was so scared he would try to hurt you."

"You, scared?"

"Where you're concerned, yes." He rested his cheek against her hair, his shaky sigh disturbing the tiny curls at her ear. "I was coming up the aisle to confront him. Then you let him sit down, and all I could think was that he could hurt you before I could stop him. That's when I started praying."

Katie's heart shifted inside her chest. He had prayed for her. She would always love him, as she had most all her life. And if he didn't return her love, she would mourn, but she would survive.

Because she had been chosen by God.

"Katie?"

She wanted to ignore him, to bury deeper into his arms for just one more moment longer, but it would only make it more difficult to let him go. Katie relaxed her grip on his lapel.

But Josh didn't relax his hold on her; his lips gently brushed against her ear. "I would never consider a job as the town doctor without first talking with you."

Katie lifted her head. "You wouldn't? Why?"

Josh's gaze traced the line of her jaw, paused for a long moment on her lips before meeting her gaze. "You really have no idea how wonderful you are, do you, Katie? Because you are, you know. And intelligent and giving. Which is why Etheridge is offering you a position as one of the town's doctors."

"One of?"

"Two. Me and you."

"A partnership? Etheridge said that?"

Josh nodded. "Yes. And I agreed only if you are the senior partner."

Her eyes glittered with unshed tears. "You would do that for me, Josh? Make me the senior partner? Why?"

"For a lot of reasons, but mainly because you are a very fine doctor and I want people in this town to respect that. Life changes, and people have to go along with it. To every purpose, there is the season, and I want to be here when your season comes."

"But what about Kansas? You were itching to go out West."

"I sent a telegram to them telling them I couldn't take the job." Josh leaned forward, his lips brushing a soft kiss against her forehead. "Not when I want to stay here. With you."

Her heart fluttered wildly in her chest, but then she remembered his reason for being in Hillsdale in the first place. "What about the marriage contract?"

"I've been thinking about that," Josh said, his arm tightening around her shoulders until the tip of her nose barely touched his. His eyes met hers and held. "Why don't we abide by the contract?"

"What?" Katie pressed her palms against his chest, ready to fly off the handle until she felt the ripples of laughter beneath her fingers. So, he thought he could tease her? Well, he was sadly mistaken. She slid her arms around his neck. "I'm glad that's settled."

"I'm sorry." A gentle smile lit up his features, his free hand coming up to caress the tender line of her face. "I shouldn't tease you like that. Truth is, that contract has been null and void since right after Mother died."

She didn't know why, but a vague sense of disappointment flowed through her. "You mean you came all this way for nothing?"

Josh trapped her chin between his fingers. "No, it's not..." He hesitated. "Our fathers didn't draw up that contract. My mother asked your father to draw it up while she was dying. She probably figured out I was a little in love with you even then. But when your father took the position here at the college, she saw the contract as an opportunity for us to find out if what we felt for each other was real. Father only told me the contract was legal to follow through with her dying wish."

Katie could only focus on the words that made her heart burst with happiness. "You loved me even then?"

"Just a little," he teased before growing serious again. "I think that's why things were so awkward between us that last year. I didn't know how to handle all those feelings I had for you."

"I didn't either," she confessed. "I blush thinking about all the silly ways I tried to get you to notice me."

"It was probably a good thing your father brought you to Hillsdale. Gave us time to grow up a little, figure things out about ourselves." Josh leaned closer, his face blurring slightly until her eyes drifted shut. "I love you, Katie."

"I love you, too," she whispered against his lips.

He kissed her then, his mouth clinging to hers in a long-awaited welcome. It was their season now, a time to love.

* * * * *